LETTERS FROM BLITZ

DAN SANTOS

A Novella

Dedicated to you, if you ever loved a dog.

TABLE OF CONTENT

ONE

Blitz couldn't move and he hated that. His belly hurt. He couldn't feel his legs. In his mind, he had turned weak and ugly, the total opposite of what he used to be. He hated being at the mercy of bodily functions he once set aside for the backyard. Mommy and Daddy had to clean up after him. They had to carry him everywhere. What kind of life was this?

The pain was real. He could not stretch out his legs to lessen the pain that pierced his tummy. He couldn't go on. He caught himself hoping the end would come soon. Maybe he'd go away like Lars and Maggie. Wherever they had gone had to be better.

Daddy carried him to the deck that led to the backyard. Even for a strong guy like his human dad, Blitz's 90 pounds must have been a heavy load; a punishing task he suffered without complaint.

The man with the bundle stood by the patio door. Blitz remembered him well. It was the same man who came the day Maggie left. The roll of soft, brown cloth wrapped around the things he used on Maggie. His humans called him "doctor."

Blitz looked at the man's eyes. To him, they looked cold, malevolent. Maybe this would be the day it would all end, like it had been for Maggie.

It was awful to think he'd be leaving his humans. But he couldn't bear another day of weakness, another day of shame and pain. He just couldn't go on.

They had spread a blanket on the deck, on the same spot they had prepared one for Maggie. Changing her mind at the last minute, Mommy moved it into the family room. Maggie left in the hot days of August. February days were colder and Mommy didn't want him to be cold. She had once said she didn't fear death; just its coldness. Blitz no longer cared.

Nothing had worked. They had pushed him into machines with lots of lights and weird noises. People in white coats had stared at him, poked at his body and shaken their heads, with Daddy flinching at each jab. Some of the white-coated humans had numbed his pain and made him sleep; telling him all would be OK when he woke up. They had lied.

Daddy avoided his eyes each time Blitz sought his gaze; that gaze which had always conveyed love and tenderness. He desperately wanted his human dad to look at him so he could tell him it was OK, that he knew it was time, that he wanted it to be the end.

Knowing what Blitz wanted to tell him, his human was too smart to let their eyes meet. The man's psyche rejected the thought of Blitz's death. It was too painful to think his boy would be gone in a few minutes. He paced back and forth doing and saying things he didn't have to do or say; meaningless words and actions meant to delay the moment. His eyes seemed moist and the sniffles uncharacteristic. *Oh, Daddy, if you only knew how much I love you and Mommy.*

For the millionth time Blitz wished he could make human sounds. He understood what humans told him, but they did not understand his growls, barks, howls and whimpers.

The two humans who meant the world to him kneeled by his side, stroking him, holding him tighter than he could stand. The man with the bundle crouched in silence, unrolled the cloth and selected a shiny thing from it. He drew liquid from a small bottle, looked at it against the light and pushed the plunger until a drop appeared on its pointy end. In one smooth motion the man slid the needle into Blitz's neck and pushed the plunge. Warm liquid rushed through him. Growing tired, he at last held the eyes of his humans.

The liquid warmed his insides. It felt good. Sleep came and the light dimmed. The last thing he experienced was his human family holding on to him even harder than before; their tears wetting his fur; their voices telling him they loved him.

When the gloom reached its darkest shade, it turned abruptly into a white light so brilliant that it hurt the eyes.

Blitz blinked and looked around. It was intensely white, fluffy, and cottony. He floated. Hovering above clouds gave him a thrilling new perspective. In a moment of clarity he sensed the pain had left him. It was all gone. Gliding aimlessly gave him a sense of wellbeing. Wait until they saw him!

Hold it! They would see him, right? Where were they? All he saw was clouds. He felt good, but not seeing anyone around was frightening.

He'd had enough. Shaking his floppy ears he stretched his legs and straightened his spine. His feet patted the soft surface; first with caution, then with more confidence. It had been so long since last his legs held him upright. For a moment, he thought he would stumble and fall, but he didn't. Taking a tentative step and then another, he moved forward. Yes! He could walk again.

Emboldened, he willed his still stiff extremities to move faster. They responded and he took off like a young pup.

Wait! His brain shrieked a warning. It was great to run again, but where was he running to? The initial momentum kept him going. Narrowing his hazel eyes he focused on a far-away spot in the sea of white and fluffy substance. The dark spot stood in contrast to the clouds. As he neared it, it turned lighter, sort of greenish, until it became a full array of greens, browns and grays.

Bounding forward, a puppy grin transformed his expression. His front legs sprung and landed playfully in a crouch. That's how he used to tease and play when younger. It had been so long ago.

Impatient, he sprinted ahead, nose pointed toward the rapidly defining target, sniffing to capture its scent, eyes clasped on its mystery. The brownish-green was now a hill. With a mind of their own, his legs brought the mad dash to a halt.

An ocean of clouds encircled the hill and everything as far as he could see. The mound resembled an island sprouting out of a misty sea. Audaciously ascending, his foot pads felt the moist, green grass. A feeble breeze caressed and cooled his nostrils. It smelled great.

Then it dawned on him he had darted up the hill without once huffing and puffing; just like the old Blitz before he got sick. But the place looked weird.

Reaching the hill's crest, Blitz scanned for other elevations, but saw only other dark spots in the distance. Loneliness clutched his heart when he thought those spots might only be other disappointing mounds like this one; just hills, nothing else. Where is everyone?

Before, he'd only felt this alone when imprisoned in the plastic crate within the flying machine that took him to faraway places. But he'd never felt this lonely. At least, the flying machine made an awful racket to keep him company. Plus, he knew Mommy and Daddy sat above the cargo area, waiting to hold him and kiss him when it got to wherever.

Something startled him on the left: a square and still ill-defined shape. In an impulse, he ran to where the smoky whiteness melted into the structure.

Once closer, Blitz thought his eyes were playing tricks. It looked like someone had thrown a roof on a road. No walls, just a magical darkness holding up the roof. But it wasn't a normal roof. An incredible display of brightly colored rays sprouted from its top. He'd never seen so many hues of reds, blues and yellows. They turned deeper, sharper, as he got closer. There were so many beautiful colors.

Following a mysterious urge, he ran toward it until something stopped him; something he couldn't see. His nose had bumped against an unseen obstacle. Blitz lunged forward again, but it held firm. Whatever blocked him was also bouncy. It wasn't like when he bumped into furniture. It didn't hurt. He just couldn't get through.

He heard the voice.

"You can't go there yet, Blitz."

With short, staccato movements he turned his head looking for the source of the sound. It seemed to come from inside a thick, shifting cloud that seemed bulkier than the others.

Strangely compelled to respond, Blitz sensed weird sounds forming in his throat. When they came out, they were just like the ones Mommy and Daddy made.

"Why? Who are you?" He looked everywhere, alarm gripping his every cell. "Where is everyone?"

These new things seemed odd, events peculiar. The human sounds he had made added to his discomfiture.

"All in good time, Blitz."

The words reaching his ears rang soft, their tenor melodious. Soft and melodious were good, right? That shouldn't be scary, right? Breathing more evenly, his eyes bore into the slowly changing cloud, squinting and searching for whoever was talking from inside it.

"How do you know my name? And how is it I can make people sounds?"

"My name is Spirit Guide and I know everyone's name, Blitz. You will too. There will be answers to all your questions… in good time."

The cloud materialized into a tall, fawn-gray figure with hazel eyes, long ears and humongous wings sprouting from his back. Apart from the wings, it looked just like him and Maggie and the little siblings he recalled from long ago.

Now deep within the fog that challenged his composure, he paused to think about the little ones. Strange, he had not thought about his puppy siblings for a long time.

For the briefest of moments he wondered what had become of them. His impromptu ruminations drifted to the day the woman put them all in a large building with a straw floor. The horses in its stalls whinnied at the sight of the tiny puppies.

It had been fun at first. He and his siblings played all the time. And then the milk stopped.

The larger being who fed them had no more milk. She was 'milkless,' the woman had said; the woman who had turned irritable when she found out she was sick. Blitz tried to remember more, but the voice brought him back to the present.

"Welcome to the Rainbow Bridge."

TWO

Looking into Spirit Guide's big hazel eyes, Blitz felt more curious than afraid. A bright incandescence framed the apparition and its wings; a telltale sign of its importance, he thought. But despite Spirit Guide's aura of authority, the sweet tones of his speech rang reassuring; although there was a kind of sadness to them.

"Things look strange, right Blitz?"

He thought it best to not answer. Instead, he listened. He still wasn't used to the people sounds he could now make, and to be frank, making them scared him. Also, he remembered Daddy once saying to the little ones that listening was more important than talking. It helped understand things better. Plus, when people listened before speaking they made fewer mistakes. Funny how he remembered things his humans had told the little ones.

"Though it may seem you're alone, Blitz, you are not. Many here know you and love you. Your best buddy Lars is here. Maggie is also here, but she's spending time with someone from her first human family."

When Spirit Guide mentioned Lars and Maggie, Blitz's heart filled with happiness. Of course they would be here. They left before he did. He loved Lars and Maggie. He remembered fun times frolicking, running, ball chasing and rope tugging.

And then, the sum of Spirit Guide's message sunk in. Blitz's eyebrows went up and his eyes grew wider. He raised his lips, showing angry teeth. It was hard to believe the sudden rage he felt.

"You mean the people who made Maggie go away and sent her to our house so we would care for her; those humans? Is she crazy? They threw her out of their house because they thought she would hurt their new little one; as if that were possible. Maggie was the kindest being I have ever known. Kicking her out after ten whole years in their house was more than nasty. Are those the people you mean?"

"Blitz, I know how you think. That's how people on Earth would. It's different here."

He felt an incredible ire rising; like lava exploding into a volcano's crater to later spill down its sides. Its fury seeped into his head; its heat darkening his features to a deeper shade, pushing out angry words.

"Different, my butt! It was I who sat up with Maggie all those nights she cried while everyone in the house slept. She could not understand what she had done so wrong to be kicked out. It took us forever to make her feel at home after that experience. And now she's spending time with those mean people?"

"Don't worry too much about things you don't yet understand, Blitz. You'll see Maggie after a while. She's part of your family and you will all be together again. However, love is what counts the most at the Rainbow Bridge. Those other humans loved her once, not in the same way you and your human parents loved her. But they loved her in their own way. Maggie is with one of them now and he is telling her how sorry he is.

"You may not believe this, but Maggie still feels for them. She's assuring him she's not angry; that she knows anyone can make a mistake. You and I can also be wrong. Almost all beings can be wrong. You'll get to appreciate that too."

Rather than continuing to confront Spirit Guide, Blitz shut up, but not before one last headstrong swipe at the Maggie argument. He spat out the still strange human sounds.

"I'm not sure I'd have it in me to forgive Maggie's first family. I really dislike meanness."

True to his tolerant nature, Blitz's anger made a quick exit. He released it with a sigh. He shook the floppy ears with finality and turned away from Spirit Guide, his eyes settling on a distant point on the horizon to avoid looking at the imposing figure. The little voice inside him told him it would be better to let Spirit Guide talk and not to upset him. He would ponder about all this later, when alone.

Spirit Guide fixed his gaze on him; eyes mirroring the tenderness of his words.

"Like I said, you'll understand everything in good time. First, you need to learn the rules."

The base of Blitz's long ears perked up at the 'R' word, eyes growing wide and expectant. *Oh no, they have those here too!*

He remembered the first time he'd heard the 'R' word. It had to do with not making water inside the house. Mommy, Daddy and the little ones had all shrieked at once and rushed him to the yard when his bladder let go. The rule said it was OK to make water in the grass, but not inside the house.

Obeying rules didn't come naturally. He would get sad when they scolded him for breaking rules; even rules that didn't make sense to a puppy. He let out a sigh of relief when Spirit Guide said he would explain the rules and also the reasons for having them. That was a heck of a lot better than the first time they gave him rules to live by.

The mentor chose his words carefully, conscious that soft words were easier on a restless spirit. Blitz appreciated Spirit Guide's softening his tone. Soft worked better than hard. Full understanding would come much later, after he had a chance to think about what the words meant. He guessed he'd have to be patient. His humans once told the little ones that patience made problems simpler to fix.

Spirit Guide mentioned the name of this strange place again: The Rainbow Bridge. *Of course! That explained the colors shooting up from the roof on that covered road.* But he didn't quite remember the road crossing a river. Weird!

He also told Blitz many of those who waited for their reunions at the Rainbow Bridge did so for a long time.

"But why wait? Why not make it happen right away?"

"Think about it, Blitz. You had to die before you came here, so must your loved ones. No one gets here until they fulfill their purpose."

More heavy words.

"Do you mean I didn't come up here until I had fulfilled my purpose?"

11

"Precisely, young man."

"And what was that?"

"Some people say dogs were put on Earth to teach humans how to love unconditionally. They are not wrong, but there's more to it."

His human dad had long conversations like this with him when there was no one around. Blitz loved those moments. He may not have understood all the words, but they made him comfortable.

One time, Daddy told him there was a purpose, a reason for everything, even when it wasn't clear right away.

Another evening, as he sat next to his human mom, she told Blitz she loved how he looked deep into her eyes just before he curled up next to her. She hugged him really tight; the first of many hugs she would give him. Maybe that's what Spirit Guide meant by loving unconditionally.

"Sometimes good people do bad things without meaning it. A friend can help them follow the good path with a look, a word, even a shrug; and some times, with his silence.

"A dog can remind his humans they need to do what's good with a head tilt and a meaningful gaze. Head tilts can handle small issues, like not making water inside the house, and big things, like not hurting someone else without a good reason."

Blitz looked up at Spirit Guide's face with renewed interest, eager to hear the point the daunting figure was trying to make.

Instead, Spirit Guide switched to explaining the different kinds of 'hurt.' Changing tracks annoyed Blitz, but he knew it was important to let the mentor make his point.

"Many arrive at the Rainbow Bridge after someone or something hurt them; whether pain was in their bodies or in their minds. 'Body hurt' is easier to understand than 'mind hurt.'"

Blitz knew 'body hurt' first hand. He understood humans could fix some pains but not others.

"'Mind hurt,' however, is harder to fix. While there is no 'body hurt' at the Rainbow Bridge, everyone arrives with 'mind hurt.' So, they made most rules to deal with 'mind hurt' while waiting for the day their humans came to collect them."

Spirit Guide went on there would be some 'mind hurt,' such as not being able to see his friend Lars until the oldest little one came to collect him.

Blitz's attention strayed momentarily as he considered how he still thought of them as 'the little ones,' despite their now being adults, caring for their own little ones. His attention snapped back when Spirit Guide explained his main job was to lessen 'mind hurt.'

Spirit Guide clarified that breaking the rules disappointed him, and Rainbow Bridge denizens would not want to do that. They would feel guilty, and guilt caused 'mind hurt.' The jaded part of Blitz's personality thought the explanation was somewhat self-serving–but he kept it to himself.

Spirit Guide had caught a meaningful head tilt earlier, when he mentioned Lars. Building on Blitz's interest, he explained the Rainbow Bridge was a point of reunion. 'Mind hurt' would go away the day they reunited with their loved ones. Until then, there would be ways to lessen the 'mind hurt' of not seeing Lars and Maggie physically.

Taking the furry mentor's opening, he tilted his head.

"So what could lessen the 'mind hurt' of not seeing them?"

"Letters; you will be able to communicate with them through magical letters."

Blitz's eyes brightened.

Until the reunion Blitz could 'talk' to others at the Rainbow Bridge using 'letters.' They would write and send these 'letters' with their thoughts, not with paper, ink and stamps, as people did on Earth. Blitz was ecstatic, but he still had questions.

"So, when can I start to send them letters?"

His ears flopped in disappointment when Spirit Guide told him once again 'all in good time.'

Although he was fiercely independent and a bit of a rebel, Blitz remained quiet and respectful. He did not want to tell his mentor that having to wait sucked. At that thought, he saw Spirit Guide smile. The smile told him his mentor had dealt with frustration before. It also told him he might have something else to worry about. Could Spirit Guide read his mind?

THREE

When Spirit Guide walked away, Blitz strolled to one of the shade trees on the hill. He and Lars had loved to sit and think things through while curled under a tree in the backyard; a kind of tree humans called 'willow.' Its branches were droopy and moved soothingly with the breeze. The swaying of the willow's branches calmed their restless spirits and stimulated their imaginations.

Not all the shade trees on the hill looked like the willow in the backyard, but his new tree's hanging boughs came close. Its homey feeling gave him a respite from the intense, shapeless whiteness; making him comfortable enough to reflect on this magical place.

Blitz knew Spirit Guide had limited that first session to just a few of the many promised rules. He was certain he would have to learn many more. Curiously, the furry mentor had not said what would happen if someone broke the rules. Blitz wondered what would happen to someone who found the rules annoying and disregarded them; he, for instance. The thought made him uncomfortable.

It was a real stomper. Should he be afraid of being punished for breaking a rule? Something didn't compute. If Spirit Guide thought love and kindness were so important, how could he do something bad to someone who broke the rules? Blitz thought his mentor had left huge gaps in the information he gave him.

For one thing, he hadn't said precisely 'when' he would be allowed to send a letter to Lars and Maggie. Why not now? What could happen?

Filled with resolve, he wrote a first letter in his head.

My dearest Lars:

I'm very excited! I can finally get in touch with you.

That also means I'm here, at the Rainbow Bridge.

Of course, you are probably aware of that. You've been here longer than me. You must know everything about this place.

I'll write longer letters after I find out whether this 'letter' thing actually works. It's not the same as talking with you, but it's better than nothing. At times, while I was down on Earth, I would sense your presence. At those times I would imagine us chasing squirrels or examining a strange smell under a fallen tree, like we used to do.

Thinking you were around me was good. But it wasn't the same as actually having you there. It's been so long since I heard from you. I can't wait to get your news.

I hope I'm not breaking a rule writing to you before Spirit Guide's 'all in good time' caution. If this works, I'll tell you more about him later. I just want to know how you are doing and what you think of the Rainbow Bridge. To me, everything is more than weird.

Please answer quickly and tell me how you are doing. I miss you so much.

Love,

Blitz

A whoosh startled him the moment he signed his name to the mental letter. Thinking about it, the sound reminded Blitz of the noise speeding cars make. So, it was both startling and scary. He guessed he would get used to it.

Despite the mystery surrounding the process, he was almost sure he had sent his first letter. Also, he supposed it would take some time to get an answer from Lars. So he dropped down under the tree to wait.

Killing time, he mulled over whether this ability to write letters in your mind worked only here at the Rainbow Bridge. Wouldn't it be great if he could also send a letter to Mommy and Daddy to tell them not to worry; that he was OK? He found it infuriating to not understand everything.

Suddenly, he heard another whoosh and something wonderful happened: his head filled with words.

My dearest, dearest Blitz:

When I heard the incoming whoosh, I got as excited as the day my Mommy first gave me "the funky chicken." You remember that's how she used to call that funny rubber toy I used to play with? Anyway, I was really thrilled.

I'm sad and happy at the same time. I'm happy because I finally get to write letters with you. And I'm sad, because your being here means you may have hurt before you came. You may have figured out by now that when we are here we don't know for sure about sad things that happen on Earth, although there is no rule that says we can't guess.

I hope you didn't hurt too much; and of course I mean 'body hurt.' I guess you may have had a lot of 'mind hurt.'

I also hope someday we can have long talks face to face again; just like we did when we lived together. I need to look at your eyes. Most folks don't know that we say a lot with our eyes.

Well, I guess the good news is we are together again.

Please, tell me everything that happened since the last time we saw each other. Tell me also about your human parents. And, most of all, I'd love to know how my Mommy is doing. I miss her so much. I can't wait to see her again. Well, I don't really mean that. I'd hate for her to die just so we can reunite here. Oh, I'm not sure what I mean. You remember my Mommy thought I was a scatter-brain! I guess it's true.

Please write me quickly!

Love,

Lars

As he read Lars' response, a nearby whoosh told Blitz someone may have sent a letter. Did the sound mean Lars was close by? Would he hear whooshes when everyone wrote letters? That could prove annoying.

He had many questions about the Rainbow Bridge. But he didn't want to ask too many at once to avoid hearing Spirit Guide's vexing 'all in good time.'

Pondering about Rainbow Bridge letters, he suddenly became aware of the many whooshes going off around him. Much later, he would learn he would only hear those whooshes that concerned him.

But, there it was! Lars had answered. This 'letter thing' really worked. He supposed he could now start writing about important stuff; stuff that really mattered to him.

My Lars:

I'm so excited! Letters do work! So I'll begin at the beginning, like my human dad used to say.

First, your Mommy is fine. She wasn't fine when you first came up here. She cried a lot. And my Daddy cried when she called to tell him you had passed. He was shocked at your death. His heart ached because he loved you and knew of our great friendship, and that your absence would make me miserable.

My Mom also cried a lot while holding me, thinking I could die too. She would hold on to me so hard it hurt. And the sobbing seemed to have no end. No matter how hard my human dad tried, there was no consoling them.

Holding on to your Mommy, they cried until all the tears dried up. I once heard someone say mothers and daughters share one heart, and I guess it's true. You remember your Mommy is my mom's eldest daughter, right?

I shudder to think about that day; especially the moment I realized I would not see you again. It made me question whether loving someone is a good thing. But I guess never loving someone can be worse. I have had so many confusing thoughts, but I'm here with you now.

Let's move to more practical matters. This guy Spirit Guide I wrote about is someone who looks just like me. He is trying to teach me things about the Rainbow Bridge. While he scared me at first, I've gotten used to him. He sounds smart and caring, and interested in making me feel good. But he's going so slowly!

When I get impatient and ask questions he's not ready to answer he tells me 'all in good time.' Lars, I think it's so annoying to wait for answers. I guess you know I don't have much patience.

But, wait, I'm not answering your question about what all happened after you left.

We moved to another house where there were many trees and lots of room to run. I wish you had been there. It seemed so big for me alone.

A while after we moved to the new house, a man brought someone named Maggie to live with us. She looked a lot like me, but she was older. And Lars, she was a girl! Of course I had seen girl dogs before, but I had never lived with one. I didn't know what to expect.

It wasn't a happy thing at first. For the longest of times she looked so sad. She started to look sad the day her human left her with us. She ran after him as far as the fence would let her, but he got into his car and drove away.

I saw the car stop a short distance away, as if the human had changed his mind and wanted to return for Maggie. I could have sworn he was looking at her from far away. Maggie also noticed the car stop. In her eyes, I saw the hope the man had changed his mind. I guess she was anticipating his coming back to get her. The car sped away and she hung her head in defeat.

A little while ago Spirit Guide told me someone from Maggie's first human family arrived, and she had asked to meet with him for a short time. He said he allowed it with the understanding that Maggie is part of our family and she would reunite only with our human parents when either of them gets here.

At first it made me angry, and I guess I'm still irritated. But Spirit Guide tells me we should not think or feel about things in the same way we did on Earth. Our thoughts at the Rainbow Bridge should be kinder.

I'm still upset about it, so I'm going to stop here, take a nap and calm down. I'll write some more later.

I kiss you.

Blitz

FOUR

Blitz awoke dazed and bewildered. Had he dreamed about the Rainbow Bridge, Spirit Guide, the lectures on the rules and even the letters; or, were these things part of a convoluted nightmare? He wanted to think they were not real because, if they were, it meant his time on Earth had ended.

Sadly, the grass tickled his feet when he walked over it; the tree seemed solid enough when he leaned against it; and the sea of clouds surrounding the hill fluttered with the breeze. What's more, there was no denying Lars' letters sounded real.

This was his new, unsatisfactory and depressing reality. Writing letters was great. It filled the void of not knowing how Lars and Maggie were doing. But what bothered him the most was thinking Mommy and Daddy would be worried about him. Blitz knew how they would be suffering not knowing how he was doing at the Rainbow Bridge; or that this place existed at all.

Maybe there were other things he wasn't super happy about, but not being able to reassure his human mom and dad was up there on the list. The obvious solution - sending them a message - seemed impossible from what he knew about this place and its rules. It was as maddening as scratching an itch in one of his ear folds.

His instinct told him there might be a rule against contacting his humans. It also told him Lars's experience at the Rainbow Bridge could be the key to finding a way to go around such a rule. The problem was Lars had a keen sense of 'right and wrong.' If he thought it would be wrong to break that rule, he would not help Blitz. So, he would have to approach Lars carefully.

My Dear Lars:

I ended my last letter telling you how Maggie came to stay with us, and how sad she was at first. It's hard for me to write about things and then wait to hear what you have to say. I would much rather sit with you under a tree and talk. Though sometimes you would scold me for some of my wild ideas, I know you'd have my back.

Spirit Guide hasn't been around since we've started writing letters, so I haven't had a chance to ask him questions. But I have you. I love you and I trust you.

Sometimes, his reluctance to answer my questions right away leaves me dissatisfied and worried about breaking rules and displeasing him. I would much rather ask you so I could interrupt you and ask you about things I don't quite understand. I don't feel too comfortable interrupting Spirit Guide. For all I know, there could be a rule against that! I don't want to get in trouble.

After you left for the Rainbow Bridge, we moved to the big house I told you about. There may have been many reasons for moving, but I've always suspected the most important one was to forget sad things that happened in that apartment we shared.

The big house had a large, fenced-in backyard covered with soft grass. There was also a big wooden deck with a brick barbeque to cook yummy meats when people came to visit. The house had an upstairs, a downstairs and a basement; so you can imagine how many steps we had to climb to go up and down. Well, that's where we lived when Maggie came.

I told you how her old family had thrown her out of their house and how sad she was. It was all I could do to calm her down. Although she was older than me, I managed to get her to play a little. I thought playing might take things off her mind. I would prance by her with a big toy rope, and after a while she would chase me and tugged at the rope with me.

But every night, when we were all supposed to be asleep, I could hear her whimpering softly on her cushion.

Mommy also tried to lessen her sadness. She'd take us to nearby woods by a creek so we could run around and chase deer. Exploring the woods distracted her for a while, but there was no making Maggie happy. It got to a point my humans decided to take her to the doctor because she looked really sick. She even had trouble walking.

The doctor gave us bad news. He told us her internal organs were failing and it was only a matter of time until she would be gone. That really depressed me, but I hid it because I knew Daddy and Mommy would not want Maggie to see us sad.

Then, some of Mommy's relatives came to visit. I'll never forget it. Daddy will never forget it either. Their kids started making fun of how Maggie couldn't walk right. I had never seen my human dad so angry. He told the kids' parents it wasn't right to make fun of the sick; that people who did that showed they weren't good people. The kids' mother scolded them, but the harm was done.

Shortly after mom's relatives left, Maggie got to the point where she couldn't walk at all, and she would eat less each day. My humans cried every night, knowing what they had to do. The doctor they called had a brown cloth bundle in his hand; a bundle I would never forget. He shook his head and told them he agreed the only thing he could do was to stop her pain and let her die in peace.

Mommy and Daddy cried, but in the end they couldn't see her suffer any more and let the man put a needle into her to help her cross the Rainbow Bridge.

The night she came to the Rainbow Bridge, we all stayed awake with the inert Maggie. The next day, Daddy took her away and returned with a little box that had Maggie's ashes in it.

Every night Daddy would look at the box and cry remembering Maggie. It was all so sad.

I'll write more later because I'm too sad right now.

I love you,

Blitz

Blitz shut his teary eyes and tried to sleep. Sleep would not come easy when he was sad or worried. He made himself recall how Maggie was now pain free. His eyelids grew heavier. Breathing became louder and more regular. He was almost there when an incoming whoosh sprung his eyes open.

My Blitz:

I felt the sadness in every word you wrote. It made me very sad too.

Maggie had already written me about the story from her point of view. You have no idea how much she loved you and your human parents for being so kind to her.

She told me she was relieved and thankful when they put an end to her suffering. She also said she couldn't wait to see your human parents, and to tell them how much she loved them, and how their decision to end her pain was a good thing.

You should know the decision humans make to end our pain is one of the biggest issues at the Rainbow Bridge. It's not so much the decision, but the suffering our humans go through afterwards. If they only knew how we appreciate the love it takes to see it through.

I will write Maggie to let her know you're here and you can then write to each other. I'm sure she'll be happy at the news, despite the sadness of it all. As to her visiting with the guy from her first family, it's complicated, Blitz. Spirit Guide is right. Things are different here; difficult to understand sometimes, but different.

When I first got here someone came to mentor me also, except he looked like me, not you. His brown and black coloring was the same, as well as the bent ears and black eyes of a German Shepherd mix. The scuttlebutt is Spirit Guide makes himself look like the one he's talking to. I think he does it to gain your trust.

But really, he is very kind, and he means well. He tells you all these things to help you get along in this strange place; you know, to make you comfortable. Some of us have to wait for a long time until we see our loved ones again. That's the worst thing about the Rainbow Bridge.

Don't get upset with me, but I think Spirit Guide is right: things will be clear 'in good time.' I fully understand your impatience because I am also a little impatient. But what can I do? I don't want to see my Mommy again soon if it means it will make her hurt to leave her life on Earth. On the other hand, I would love to feel her arms around me again.

Please keep telling me about your life on Earth. It means so much to me, even if some things make me sad.

I send you a big sloppy kiss.

Lars

FIVE

The little hairs on Blitz's neck would bristle with each whoosh. On Earth, bristling meant he was ready to fight. At the Rainbow Bridge, it was due to excitement, uncertainty and even a little fear. Was the whoosh for him? Was it for someone else? Would that letter bring good news?

He knew instinctively the sound would become routine in time, and that he would hardly notice it. But that was not the case now. Whooshes made his heart jump. It was also an incredible rush; an indeterminate emotion which would prove to be the harbinger of his greatest discovery.

My dear Lars:

There is a thought trying to break through my consciousness; like when you have an answer on the tip of your tongue and it won't come out. I'll let you know when it comes out. In the meantime, let me tell you the story of how we found out I was sick.

Some people thought it was sad, but I've never liked to wallow in self-pity. In fact, my human dad once told me they bred Weimaraners to protect German forest keepers from bears and wild boar. Someone as brave as that will not allow sadness to cloud his spirit or his letters. So, I won't.

Shortly after Maggie passed, Mommy was walking with me when she started looking closely at the water I was making to mark a tree. We kept walking, but I saw her stare each time I stopped. Her face turned serious, like when I would do something wrong. But when I looked up at her–searching for clues or forgiveness—she would only smile and pat my head; like reassuring me I hadn't done anything wrong.

A few days later I walked into the house from the backyard with my back bent and my rear legs shortened by the effort. It was a Sunday, so Dr. Andrews wasn't in his office and my humans took me to another doctor who poked me and put me under a machine. He told them he thought I had hurt my back. Mommy and Daddy sighed with relief that it was something that could be helped.

You may also remember my Mommy liked to be what she called 'thorough;' what my dad laughingly called 'a thorough pain in the butt.' The next day she took me to ask Dr. Andrews if the other doctor had been right—I'm sure you remember Dr. Andrews helped end your pain. After he helped you cross, I always worried when I went to see him. I was also secretly angry at him for sending you here because I didn't understand many things then.

Dr. Andrews drew blood and looked at it. He told Mommy and Daddy I had something called 'cancer,' which is a pretty bad illness. But he wanted to give them hope, so he sent me to a bigger place with many doctors and machines. They said Dr. Andrews was right.

My humans talked on the telephone with many other doctors to see if they could cure me. There was some hope in a place called Chicago, where a doctor was doing cancer research. But they all agreed my illness was too advanced for the new treatment to cure me.

There came another mad rush to places and machines when my legs began to drag as I walked. More places and machines took over when I could no longer walk. Dad even brought me a cart with wheels to help me walk.

They tried everything. Daddy took me to a place he used to go on Sundays to pray to someone he called God. There, he asked a person he called a Priest to help him find the right words to ask God for help.

The man told him it was not possible to ask God to help a dog. He said dogs' souls were not as good as the souls of human beings, so he couldn't ask God for help. Dad was furious at the man's answer. Later, he would say terrible things about those who claimed to speak in the name of God. He had spent his entire life trusting those people who now refused to help me.

I had never seen Mommy and Daddy so desperate. They wouldn't cry in front of me but I heard my dad once beg God to prove his love for him by curing me. It turns out Daddy should not have spoken to God that way. One of God's rules was to never tempt Him. You see, God loved people so much that to ask Him to prove it was to tempt Him; a very bad thing.

When the doctors could not give them more hope and told them how I was suffering they decided to help me end my pain, and they called the same doctor who helped Maggie. It was a very sad day for them; sadder because they weren't sure they were doing the right thing.

So, that's how I got here. I can't believe how much they suffered for me.

Write you later,

Blitz

Blitz felt emotionally drained. He shook his ears, circled two or three times and dropped on the shady spot under the tree. Soon his eyes closed into a dreamless sleep. Only one thought crossed his mind as he drifted off. He had to tell Daddy and Mommy they had not done anything wrong. Asking the Doctor to help him die was the kindest thing they had ever done. He had no idea how he could get that message to them. Maybe Lars could help, willingly or not.

Blitz woke at the sound of an incoming whoosh.

Dear Blitz:

I am so sad you suffered.

Soon I will share your letter with Maggie, but there is a rule we can't disturb anyone who's reuniting with their families.

I, too, feel weird calling those people Maggie's family. But then, it's important to Maggie to let them know she forgives them; and to explain she wishes to wait for her real family. At least that's what Spirit Guide told me when I asked. He said they had made an exception in her case and let her have two reunions instead of just one because her first family needed to end their anguish at what they had done.

Sometimes I don't understand how things work, but I trust Spirit Guide.

Don't be sad, Blitzy. At the Rainbow Bridge we try to not be sad. Things will work out.

I love you,

Lars

Blitz had tears in his eyes when he finished Lars' letter. He dried them quickly so that Spirit Guide couldn't tell he'd been crying. Crying would embarrass him, and maybe even get him in trouble. Sure enough, when he looked up, he saw the furry mentor standing right in front of him.

"Blitz, what's the meaning of this? I've told you that we are not supposed to be sad at The Rainbow Bridge. This is a place where we prepare for the happiest event in the universe: getting back together with the people we loved more than our own lives. Fretting about it makes Love Giver sad."

The new name, Love Giver, took Blitz by surprise. It was the first time Spirit Guide mentioned someone he worried about pleasing. Blitz would have been more intrigued about Love Giver, but it sounded suspiciously like the being Daddy had called God. Above all, he was glad his mentor seemed to care about someone. It made him more normal.

Normal or not, he hoped this magical creature had not discovered the scheme that was taking shape in his mind.

SIX

Spirit Guide's scolding convinced Blitz he could wait no longer. His mentor was right. There was too much at stake. What good was it to wait for the happiest moment in anyone's life while the other person suffered? He had to contact Mommy and Daddy, no matter what. The thought they were suffering on his account was unbearable. They had done the right thing asking the Doctor to help him end his suffering, and that was that.

The task ahead was monumental. The odds were stacked against Blitz. There was a lot he didn't know about the Rainbow Bridge. So he needed more data about this place NOW!

Lars and Maggie could help, but they worried too much about getting in trouble. Lars' cautious letters made clear getting help from him would be dicey. Maggie's innate goodness would also be an obstacle to breaking whatever communication rules he had to break. He would have to trick them into helping. However, he would have to be stealthy because they were no dummies.

Spirit Guide was also a danger. Not only was he smart, but he had the power to punish Blitz if he broke any rules.

Blitz also worried Spirit Guide could read his mind. Not knowing all the rules made it difficult to sort out things that could get him in trouble. And he had to consider yet another factor. Could Spirit Guide or Love Giver read his letters?

He wrote a quick note to Lars.

Dearest Lars:

Do you know if someone else can read our letters?

Love,

Blitz

He waited what seemed like a lifetime for Lars' answer. No choice. Blitz had to fight his impulsive nature because so much depended on the answer.

Hi, Blitzy.

I'm sort of afraid to answer your question. I remember when you used to ask questions like that, out of the blue. Your innocent sounding questions would tell me you were planning to do something that could get us in trouble. I guess we don't change all that much when we come to The Rainbow Bridge.

For what it's worth, let me put your mind at ease. When he was telling me about the rules, Spirit Guide made a big deal about how he trusted everyone's good judgment in not breaking them. That's why they made the letters private.

Knowing you, you'd think he could be tricking us. But, really, I don't think he has the time to be reading everyone's letters.

By the way, Maggie just dropped me a note she had finished with her first family. I told her about you being here and she said she would write you as soon as she recovered from the visit's stress. So expect a letter from her.

I send you a hug.

Lars

Wow! This was good stuff. Not only could he almost trust Spirit Guide would not read his letters, but Maggie would write soon, too!

Blitz shook his ears and readied for action. Despite all assurances, the situation called for clear thinking and good planning. It was time to gather secret intelligence, whatever it took.

Dear Lars:

Spirit Guide hasn't yet talked to me about all the rules. As you might imagine, I have a bunch of questions. The most important question of all is what actually goes on when our loved ones arrive for the reunion.

Of course I can guess that they first have to die; that's the part I don't like. But, beyond that fact, have you put together what actually goes on at their arrival? How far in advance do we prepare for their arrival?

I know these questions sound weird, my Lars. You just have to trust me.

I send you a big sloppy kiss,

Blitz

Continuing his exploration, the invisible wall stopped Blitz short of the Bridge but close enough to enjoy again all the beautiful colors shooting up from its roof. He sniffed all around the barrier, but the fluffy white stuff had no scent, and no opening he could find. He stared at the terrain leading to, around, and as far as he could see beyond the Bridge.

His sore nose bore out the fact the trees were solid, and not figments of his imagination. The ground was firm, but somewhat spongy. He didn't quite know how useful those two pieces of information would be, but he made sure to store them safely in his head. Nothing should be overlooked.

Distances were real, too. He remembered when he first arrived and saw the green hill in the distance. Blitz had actually gotten tired getting there. Or, was feeling tired some clever trick Spirit Guide had devised? He shook his ears loudly to remind himself to not become paranoid. Daddy had once told him to accept the simplest explanations first, at least until he got more facts.

Next, he decided to get himself a safe base from which to plan and carry out the reconnaissance. That was easy. Spirit Guide had not disturbed him at all while he slept under his willow. True, the tree didn't stop the letters from Lars, but that was probably a plus.

He would have to rely on his old friend for news, creative thinking and, most importantly, the calming influence Lars was famous for. Goodness! He used to calm down squirrels with his mellifluous whimpers before chasing them to have fun, not to hurt them; never to hurt them.

So Blitz returned to his tree and meditated until Lars' letter arrived.

Dear Blitz:

I'm more convinced than ever that you are planning something, and I shudder to think about it. I know you well enough to mistrust the questions you ask, no matter how innocent they seem. I'm scared of what trouble you are going to get us into. But I'll play along. After all, the Rainbow Bridge could use some excitement while we wait for our reunions.

I looked through my letters to refresh my memory, since I had many of the same questions when I first got here. Oh, yes, you should know you always keep your letters in the back of your mind to reread them when you get bored, or remember things accurately so you can answer other letters. So, I just went through all of them to try to answer your questions.

First, there are only bits and pieces about actual arrivals. Maggie helped the most since she just came back from reuniting with her first family. However, you should know she had curiously forgotten many details when she returned from that visit. It's as if the system is rigged to make you forget things should you return here after an arrival. Sometimes reunions do not complete because the loved one who was dying gets pulled back to life for some reason. My buddies said that could happen.

But Maggie wrote me a voice called her name and told her to go to the Bridge. She also remembers the invisible wall opening for her, and that it took some time to get to the arrival place beyond the Bridge, mainly because you walk so slow in the dark.

Second, I've heard rumors that once you meet your loved ones you never come back here but go with them to some other place. Maggie sort of confirmed that point admitting

Spirit Guide had limited her visit to the area around the Bridge. She did say she felt good despite not being allowed to walk her first human father to the next place.

I'm sure you will be asking many more questions. But Blitzy, I beg you to be very careful about whatever it is you are planning to do, especially if you are going to break the rules.

No one knows what happens when you break the rules, but it can't be pleasant. I can imagine breaking the rules would make Spirit Guide angry. Tricking someone like Spirit Guide-someone who is so nice to us-cannot be good. He does not deserve to be tricked or lied to. I'm sure Love Giver should not be tricked or lied to either. Just keep that in mind.

A hug to you,

Lars

SEVEN

Blitz knew Lars would be cautious. But he did not expect his friend would use such sensible arguments to justify his caution. He no longer fit the scatter-brain stereotype he claimed.

Yes, he would have to be careful. But Lars' street smarts might come in handy. He may have been klutzy, but that was all about his body, not his brain. There was nothing klutzy about his thinking.

My dear Lars:

Thanks for the warning. I'll try to not get us into too much trouble with anyone.

Hear me out, buddy. Spirit Guide and Love Giver want us to be good, right? What if we can stop our humans from suffering needlessly for us? That's a good thing, right? Neither Spirit Guide nor Love Giver could get mad at me for trying to be good to them, right? At least I don't imagine so.

So here's what I'm thinking: There is an invisible wall that stops us from going to the Bridge, right? On this side of the wall we cannot send messages to people on Earth, right? Shouldn't we find out whether we can send messages from the other side of the wall? Maybe we could tell them we are OK and they shouldn't cry.

What do you think?

Love,

Blitz

Outgoing and incoming whooshes crossed each other.

My dearest little brother Blitz:

Lars told me you were here. While I'm happy to have you near, I hope you didn't hurt too much before you came. But I'm so happy to be able to talk with you again!

First, please tell me how Mommy and Daddy were doing when you left. I hope they are OK. You all were so good to me when I lived with you. You can't imagine how grateful I was and still am to be part of our family.

Lars also told me you didn't feel right about my having received someone from my first family. I know where you are coming from. You were always so proud and loyal!

Please understand I'm part of your family and will wait for whoever comes first. And then we will all wait together for the rest.

I knew my first family felt bad about making me go away. So, I had to tell them I didn't hold a grudge. I met my first human dad to tell him I understood why they had sent me away and that I forgave them, even if they were wrong.

Lars shared your letters with me (yes, they are private, but you can decide whether to share them with someone else), so I know a little about how you came up. I'm so happy you no longer hurt and can walk. But please, tell me how you really like it here. I know it can be strange at first, but you'll soon get to understand everything.

I hope you and I will exchange letters, like you and Lars do. Maybe we can even send group letters! What a great idea! I'll have to ask our mentor, the one you call Spirit Guide, how to do that.

I send you a big kiss,

Your sister Maggie

Blitz regretted getting mad at Maggie for visiting with her first family. Her letter made him feel warm all over. He loved that girl, yes, his sister, like she called herself. For the little time they were together on Earth they were truly brother and sister.

His soul darkened when he remembered Mommy's relatives making fun of the way her illness made her walk. Why are humans so evil?

The children laughed at her because she had to drag her legs. Daddy got red in the face and scolded the children and their parents. In response, the mother pretended to reprimand them but turned her head and smiled. Daddy caught the gesture. He never forgot their cruelty.

Out of nowhere, a thought broke his reverie. It was something Lars said in his last letter. When the voice told Maggie her first human father had arrived, how did she know they were sorry for what they had done to her? If her first family could let her know they were sorry, it means messages can get through to the Rainbow Bridge, why couldn't they also get through from the Rainbow Bridge?

Blitz knew he had to handle this latest insight carefully, so he wouldn't get Lars and Maggie in trouble with Spirit Guide, or even Love Giver. He didn't want to deceive Maggie and felt weird about asking straight out. But he thought it would be important to ask right away; before Spirit Guide let them send group letters. For sure, Lars would not approve of Blitz's planning to break the rules. So it was time to gather information from Maggie alone; what he heard call 'divide and conquer.'

My dear big sister Maggie:

I'm so happy to hear from you! The last image I have of you was Daddy and Mommy crying over your still body. I wonder if they also cried over me when I came up. Well, I'm sure they did. That's another one for Spirit Guide. He likes to tell me I will get answers 'in good time.'

Please forgive me. It was wrong to get angry for meeting someone from your first family. As you know, sometimes I'm too impulsive. I understand. I really do. Spirit Guide and Lars told me how things are different up here; how it's all about love instead of anger. So, please forgive me. You did the right thing.

How did you find out someone from your first family had arrived at the Rainbow Bridge? And, how did you find out they were sorry to have kicked you out of their house? You are right; some things up here can be weird.

Oh, Maggie, what I wouldn't give to be next to you and caress your ears like I used to do on Earth. I'd love to lie down next to you and fall asleep on the couch together, like we used to do when Mommy and Daddy went out. I never felt alone when we were together.

Okay, I'll have to stop writing about sad stuff. Spirit Guide told me we are supposed to be happy up here. But you know me. I'm not too good at following orders.

I love you Sis,

Blitz

EIGHT

Blitz hated to sit and wait. It was wasteful. He had to come up with a plan and charting his surroundings took number one priority. He made his favorite shade tree the starting point for his exploratory treks to find an easy way to go through the wall. To the casual observer the gray Weimaraner would just be sniffing around, as hunting dogs do. He knew better.

He'd keep his hazel eyes peeled for telltale signs of weaknesses on the invisible wall. Blitz had bumped his nose so many times against it that Spirit Guide had quit chiding him and reminding him that he would have to wait for that annoying 'good time.' He had confirmed the wall went all around the Rainbow Bridge like a gigantic bubble.

To save time and maintain secrecy, he composed and sent letters while moving rather than returning to his tree. Yes, it was comfortable to be at rest while he gathered his thoughts, but time was of the essence and anything that added stealth was a plus.

Blitz had reached the invisible wall's right curvature when a whoosh alerted him.

My dear Blitzy:

I was so happy to get your letter telling me you understood why I asked to visit with my first family. And I have nothing to forgive. Forgiveness is never necessary when you love someone. Love is enough.

You asked how I found out about my first family's feelings before they came up. Some of that was instinct. You know when someone you are close to is sorry about something. The other half was by accident.

When our loved ones arrive at the Rainbow Bridge, Spirit Guide opens the invisible wall enough for us to go through and greet them. It so happens I was standing near the crossing when it opened for someone. I heard and caught a glimpse of a small Schnauzer who had lived near my first family. He was rushing to his reunion.

Although I have not seen other reunions, it seems we can see others as they cross into the forbidden area and also while we are there.

As I was saying, that was the first time I had seen someone other than Spirit Guide. It startled me. I couldn't take my eyes off him as he went through the wall.

Suddenly, I heard someone crying and calling his name: Shorty. Before the wall could close on his reunion, I also heard his human telling him how happy they were to see him again. The last words I heard grabbed me hard. The Schnauzer's human said he was so happy he had always treated him with love, unlike (and he mentioned my first family's name), who had always been sorry for the way they had treated their Weimaraner girl. Now, one of them was coming to the Rainbow Bridge after a horrific car accident.

The unexpected revelation froze me in my tracks.

If they had only known how I loved little children, they would have never thought I could hurt the new baby; just because I wanted to sniff him. That was the reason they sent me away.

One thing the human said stuck in my mind: they had always been sorry for making me go away. I had been right all along.

Blitzy, I know you are new here. But Love Giver tells us to love and not judge. I had unintentionally broken that rule. I felt so sad I began to cry and recalled all the signs I should have understood.

Do you remember how my former human dad stopped his car around the corner the day he left me at your house? For a moment, I thought he had changed his mind and would return to pick me up. My heart broke when he continued driving. I don't know what I would have done if you guys hadn't been there to console me.

So I went to Spirit Guide and explained the situation. At first he said he was disappointed I had eavesdropped on something someone said in the forbidden area. But I explained it had been by accident, and that recognizing the Schnauzer had startled me. When I saw his ears drop and his eyebrows curve, I knew he had softened enough to ask for what I had in mind.

I reminded him how Love Giver asks us to love and forgive. I also said I knew the family cat would be there to greet them, but I thought they would be happy if I was there to show them I forgave them. To my surprise he agreed right away. He also asked if I wanted to stay with them instead of waiting for our Mommy and Daddy.

When I said 'oh, no' so quick and loud, he stepped back and looked deep into my eyes. Afraid to have offended him, I hurried to explain I considered Mommy and Daddy my real family because they had always shown me love. They had cared for me through my illness. I'd heard nothing but kind words while I lived with them. He softened again when I said it would only be right to repay love with love. In the end, he agreed to my plan. So here I am.

I hope this answers your question.

Love,

Maggie

Blitz's turned his gaze to a vague point over the horizon as he thought about Maggie's account. Dropping into a tight curl under his tree, he mulled over what Maggie had gone through; and how good and intelligent she was. The thought his older sister could show so much love filled him with awe. No wonder her words moved Spirit Guide to make an exception.

He was tempted for a brief moment to drop his plan to sneak out a message to his humans. Maybe, if he asked nicely, Spirit Guide would make an exception to the rules.

The thought was short lived. Who was he kidding? He was new here and Spirit Guide was no fool. Maggie deserved the mentor's love and understanding; he, Blitz, not so much. Hadn't he been quick to condemn Maggie's apparent disloyalty? That couldn't have endeared him to Spirit Guide.

Besides, Maggie had unwittingly revealed the information he needed. With a little planning and conniving he might be able to slip a message from the forbidden zone. The big question remained: would he be able to enter and leave the protected area undetected? If so, for how long?

NINE

Blitz resumed the exploration treks from his tree to the wall, not so much because they were useful to his plan. Their monotony gave him time to ponder carefully his next move.

Adding to his anxiety, there was more at stake than breaking Rainbow Bridge rules. It would be awful if Maggie found out he had tricked her into helping him break the rules. She didn't deserve to be tricked. He loved her and knew how awesome she was, and how kind she'd always been to him. It would really hurt to disappoint her.

Also, Love Giver might disapprove. Who knows what that might bring about? The being Spirit Guide seemed to obey remained a mystery to Blitz.

Just as he was about to consider whether Love Giver could be the being Daddy called God, a whoosh interrupted him.

Dear Blitz.

Maggie just told me how everything was OK between you guys again. Way to go!

It's funny how sometimes we get sad and then we change back to happy again. Thinking about it, it's just like down on Earth, except here we are happy most of the time.

At the Rainbow Bridge we know we are waiting for the happiest day of our lives; the day we reunite forever with the people we love.

This 'happy one minute and sad the next' reminds me of the story you once told me about the mamma bird. Do you remember?

You told me how you were out on a walk with your humans and a large blue bird swooped down upon the three of you. The flapping of its wings startled you, and your protective instincts made you jump up and bite it so it wouldn't harm your Mommy and Daddy. You looked at its body on the sidewalk and immediately at your humans, as if to brag how you had saved them from the attacking bird.

Then they yelled at you for doing something bad. Your Mommy walked away angry, saying she never wanted to see you again; while your Daddy said harsh words to you for having killed a momma bird who was only trying to defend her nest. You looked at them, not understanding, and quickly lowered your head and flattened your ears to let them know you were sorry.

Although eventually they forgave you, you were so confused that one moment you could be walking happily and the next sorry and sad. You told me that from that day on you turned your eyes toward them before doing anything, to check if it would be OK.

I reminded you of the story to tell you this: it's not like that at the Rainbow Bridge.

Here you learn the rules before you do anything; plus you recognize Love Giver wants you to be kind and loving to everyone. It's simple, really: if it makes Love Giver happy, you do it. If it makes him sad, you don't.

I wish it would have been so easy when we were down on Earth.

I love you, buddy.

Lars

The letter from Lars made him stop and think, if only for a brief moment.

The incident with the momma bird made him shudder each time he remembered it. It was bad enough making Mommy and Daddy angry and sad. The worst part was the realization he had ended someone's life.

It was so strange. His nature made him react in defense of his loved ones; but having killed made him sad and ashamed. He thought back at Daddy's words after he had forgiven him. There are times when it's OK to kill, and times when it is wrong.

As he recalled, it was OK to kill when someone was trying to kill you or the people you love. Yet, it was so difficult to tell when the attacker wanted to kill, or was only defending himself thinking you wanted to kill him. Then you had to decide in an instant whether to just scare him away or harm him. Sometimes rules were hard to follow.

Blitz shook his ears; not to signal beginnings and endings in the Weimaraner manner, but out of confusion. The killing conundrum made him ask himself whether it was ever OK to break Rainbow Bridge rules. For instance, would it be OK to break the rules if he did it for a good purpose?

It frustrated him things were seldom black or white; like these exploration walks he had started. Were they worthwhile? It seemed the most he got out of them was the satisfaction that, if he ever needed to recognize the terrain, he could say he had been there. But they had not helped him find out if he could send a message from the forbidden zone. Infuriating!

Lost in thought, his nose bumped into the invisible wall again; except this time it made a sound that startled him.

It couldn't have been the wall. It never made sounds before. Trying to pinpoint where the sound had come from, he caught a movement out of the corner of his eye. The wall opened, letting out a gush of air while something large and dark rushed through.

Blitz considered for a nanosecond what he'd seen. It was a big dog with brownish long hair and a happy gait. The dog's tail was about to disappear into the protected zone when Blitz made a fateful decision. He dashed in.

TEN

The air on the other side of the wall smelled different. It had the scent of freshly cut grass he remembered so well. Also, it was slightly warmer than the side where he lived.

His heart skipped a beat when he realized he'd gone through the wall without permission. He had broken the wall rule. Now what? The clear choice was to try to return to his side of the wall. However, now that he was in the forbidden zone, shouldn't he find out whether it was possible to send a message to Earth? Besides, the wall had shut behind him.

He spotted a large tree to his right and ran there, hiding behind it to buy time while he figured things out. From his vantage point he could see the big dog stepping into the covered structure. All of a sudden, he heard a happy commotion from the other side of the Rainbow Bridge.

The brown dog was making happy human sounds jumping around a man. The man cried and hugged him whenever the dog's prancing let him.

Blitz saw the man and the dog leaving the forbidden zone through another opening in the invisible wall. As he was wondering about this latest the discovery, he caught sight of more movement from the side where he had entered. Someone else was coming into the forbidden area: another reunion.

Powered by the fear of getting caught, Blitz made another split second decision. He ran through the hole back into the safe zone just as the wall closed on the new arrival.

Only when the wall had shut did it dawn on him he had not tried to send a message to his human parents. He didn't dwell on the fact he had no idea how he would have sent it. He was mortified and mentally berating himself for his clumsiness when he noticed an alarming development.

Out in the distance he could see Spirit Guide sauntering toward him. Blitz was so scared at the prospect of getting caught he felt his heart beating harder. But he decided to meet Spirit Guide head on and see what would happen. He forced his legs to move without shaking, even though he was mightily scared. Lifting his head high in a sign of recognition, he was ready to fess up the truth and tell him he was sorry.

Spirit Guide greeted him with an absentminded comment. "Oh, hi, Blitz. Listen, have you seen something strange going on? The wall sensors notified me two dogs had gone through at the same time. I came to check it out." Blitz gulped hard. The lie escaped his lips before he could think again about confessing. "No. I haven't seen anything."

The falsehood had slipped out so quickly and naturally it even surprised Blitz. Spirit Guide seemed satisfied at first blush. But the furry mentor looked pensive as he turned to resume sniffing around.

Having come close to disaster, Blitz resumed walking slowly in the direction of his favorite tree, glancing nervously everywhere except toward his mentor. Spirit Guide spoke over his shoulder. "Oh, by the way Blitz. What were you doing in this area?"

Blitz blanched. Letting out a hushed sigh, he opened his eyes wide, looking blameless and hoping he could extricate himself with another lie. "I was practicing my skills, Sir. As you know, I was a hunting dog down on Earth and we like to walk a lot."

Spirit Guide's eyes narrowed. He let his gaze fall on Blitz as he murmured softly. "I see." The counselor did not sound convinced by Blitz's hurried explanation. Nevertheless, he moved out in the wall's general direction to continue looking into the strange happenings.

By the time he was able to breathe normally again, Blitz had reached the tree and laid down, putting on an unconvincing air of innocence. He closed his eyes as if he was about to sleep, just in case Spirit Guide looked in his direction as he ambled on.

In a short while, Blitz was breathing rhythmically; the close call forgotten. He dreamed of large brown dogs.

ELEVEN

The whoosh woke him.

Dear Blitz,

Did you get my letter or were you asleep? I haven't gotten your answer.

Love,

Lars

He hurriedly searched his mind for a way to respond that didn't embarrass him or give away too much of what he was doing. The little voice in his head told him a little fib would do no harm. The other little voice reminded him Mommy once told him: 'lies are bad. After you've told the first one, you have to keep lying to cover it up.' So, he compromised, rationalizing that keeping part of the truth to himself was not lying. Right?

Dear Lars,

Sorry, you are right. I was asleep (partially true).

When I finished reading your letter I started to think about the momma bird incident and how quickly things can change from happy to sad; and, especially, how hard it is to tell right from wrong (he still wasn't lying much...but that changed with the next sentence). *And I fell asleep thinking about those things.*

(He decided to change the subject to hide the truth even deeper) *I was wondering when Spirit Guide would finish covering all the rules. Is there a special time? How long did it take him to cover them all for you?*

A big kiss,

Blitz

He hoped his not-quite-lies had warded off any suspicion Lars might have had. Sorry did not begin to describe how he felt about lying to one he loved so much. But, he was too far into this to change course.

While waiting for Lars' response to his rapidly improvised answer, Blitz took stock of the things he had found out so far:

The invisible wall opens automatically for those on the way to meet their loved ones;

There is enough time to sneak through between opening and closing;

The wall remains closed while the reunions go on.

Behind the wall, there are places to hide from whoever may be monitoring the forbidden area;

They only allow one meeting at a time; but the meetings are quick and happen in quick succession.

He had proven he could sneak in when the meeting was about to happen, but could he always return when the meeting ended?

Blitz organized all these tidbits of information in his mind, certain he could use them for developing and carrying out his plan.

Daddy once told a visitor Weimaraners were intelligent and determined. For instance, when humans used them for protection, they would lead a chasing wild boar between two closely growing trees to get them stuck.

German forest legends told of Weimaraners using their speed to run around an attacking bear. The bear standing on its hind legs would become disoriented, giving the dog the opportunity to bite its heels and make the attacker fall defeated, and at the mercy of the German foresters.

His innate cleverness told Blitz his plan was not yet complete. He was at the advance-cautiously phase. The next whoosh interrupted his train of thought.

Dear Blitz:

It's been a while since Spirit Guide had 'the rule talk' with me. But I remember he didn't get to everything right away. It took several sessions. I thought he wanted to be sure we understood the rules well. And he was a stickler for punctuality, insisting you keep the appointment as planned. He is very organized, and sharp too.

Spirit Guide makes sure you pay attention, asking you to explain back to him each rule; just to make sure you understand.

Why did you ask?

Love,

Lars

Blitz was expecting the question and had cannily put together an answer that would be mostly true and would allay suspicion, should Spirit Guide ever tell Lars of his spotting Blitz near the wall.

Instead of thinking he was being too cautious, Blitz reminded himself Lars may be big and walk funny because of his large size, but he was no dummy. It would be a mistake to underestimate him. Whatever he'd tell him should be largely true.

Dearest Lars:

I asked because I don't want Spirit Guide to be angry at me.

A little while ago I was strolling from my tree to the wall. Did I tell you that I have a favorite tree where I sleep and sit around thinking? Well, I do.

We Weimaraners like to do things in an orderly manner; probably a trait from Northern Germany, where humans developed our breed. So, I designed a pattern to explore the area. I go in a straight line from my tree to the wall until I bang my nose on it. I then return to my tree to the left of the previous trek and start on the next straight line back to the wall. Yes, I know it doesn't sound very exciting, but it fills the time while I wait for my family.

This one time I was near the wall when a big brown dog rushed through it and carried me in his wake. Imagine my surprise at being able to see someone else here! While I was still all shook up, I found myself in the forbidden zone. I tried to cross back, but the wall was shut. Thinking I had to wait for the big brown dog to go out again to sneak back into our area, I waited around, but saw him and his family go out of the zone at another point. It was too far for me to reach it before the wall closed after them.

There I was, stuck where I wasn't supposed to be and thinking about how I could call for help without getting in trouble. Just before I reached the point of desperation I noticed the wall start to open near me and another dog coming through. I didn't think twice. I pounced out of the opening just as it began to close after the dog went through. I almost missed it!

It was a close call, Lars, and I was afraid of what Spirit Guide would do to me if he found out I lied to him when he asked what I was doing there. That's why I'm asking.

A big sloppy kiss,

Blitz

TWELVE

Blitz thought his clever wording would do the job. After all, most of the explanation was true, except where it left out the real purpose for his going into the forbidden zone.

He hoped Lars and Spirit Guide would forgive him if the truth came out later. In a worst-case scenario, should Lars tell Spirit Guide what Blitz wrote, he could always apologize to both, explaining he feared angering them. He had done it out of love for his human parents.

Whoosh!

Dear Blitzy,

Oh boy, Blitz, what am I going to do with you? You could have gotten yourself in so much trouble!

It's my turn to take a nap and calm down. I also have a favorite spot near a large rock. I think I'll put it to good use.

In the meantime, please don't go getting yourself into any more trouble.

I kiss your long ears,

Lars

Wow! What luck! Not only had Lars bought his story, but he had given him a clue about his location: a large rock. He'd have to work on that.

Blitz thought the key to sending a message to Earth might be linked to the mystery surrounding the others' invisibility. It was only a gut feeling, but his greatest accomplishments came from gut feelings…well, all except the momma bird. His gut had failed him then, big time.

He had to press on.

Dear Lars,

I hope this letter doesn't interrupt your nap and you can forgive your buddy Blitz. I really didn't mean to upset you.

By the way, I'm concerned about your favorite place being near a rock. I hope it's safe. I remember how one of the little ones walked with me up a mountain not far from our house. As we walked up, I noticed some big rocks were dangerously loose. I hope you chose a safe place. I don't know if bad things can happen at the Rainbow Bridge, but let's not take any chances.

As for calming down, remember I love you. I know I get into trouble a lot, but I'm still lovable! LOL

Hugs and kisses,

Blitz

It was time to resume his walks back and forth to the wall, if for no other purpose, to keep up appearances in case Spirit Guide was watching him.

This time he added another task to his walks: spotting a big rock.

He saw it on the seventh trek: a big rock. How many of those could there be up here? The answer hit him like a kick in the gut. Looking beyond that first big rock he saw a field full of them; some bigger than others. He knew he would have to refine his indicators.

He began to draw a mental map, knowing he was pretty good at remembering details. So he pinpointed where there were long rocks, and round rocks, and rocks with other rocks on them. He knew it would take time, but it would be useful in proving his theories.

He was beat, and ready to get back to his tree when a whoosh startled him.

My dearest Blitz,

You have a knack for worrying me and then calming me down. I know you mean well but I lose sleep agonizing about you and your schemes.

Of course I chose a safe place, although I also doubt something bad could happen here. I figured a solid rock would be better than one with other rocks piled up on it. So, yeah, I picked a solid rock. It's also near a brook. The gurgling from its waters helps me fall asleep faster. It's an ideal location; especially now that you're here and I need to calm down more often.

You should try it. There must be other brooks where you are. They make this murmuring, bubbling sound that puts you at ease, and soon you forget your troubles.

I'm about to write Maggie to see how she's doing. At this time she must be curled up under her willow tree. She let me know she had chosen that tree after I told her how you and I used to love prancing around the one in your old house, playing tug with the fallen branches. Those were the days!

OK, my dearest Blitz. I'll leave you for now so I can make sure Maggie is all right.

Love,

Lars

Oh boy! Lars had given him a lot of useful information in this letter. Now he knew to look for a big rock near a brook. And, as a bonus, he had told him Maggie slept under a willow tree. How many brook and willow combinations could there be?

By the time he arrived at his tree, he had discovered hundreds of large rocks near brooks and what seemed like thousands of willows. He sighed at the thought Lars and Maggie could be anywhere near all those terrain features. But he didn't wallow in his disappointment. He bumped into Spirit Guide's soft underbelly.

"There you are, Blitz. I've been looking all over for you."

What now? Had Spirit Guide found him out?

"I think it's time to talk in depth about the rules. I usually wait a little longer, but something tells me I'd better make an exception in your case."

THIRTEEN

"Have a seat my boy. I'll tell you about each rule and then we'll discuss their meaning until I'm satisfied you understand. Our chat will be lengthy because we have a lot of rules. So, are you ready?"

Blitz snapped cheerfully. "Yes, Sir, I'm ready."

Ready? That was the understatement of the year. It was about time. He couldn't find a way around the rules unless he knew what they were.

Spirit Guide walked him to a shady spot and they sat together for what seemed like hours; the mentor rambling on, and the student trying not to fall asleep. In the end, Spirit Guide did not say anything about messaging. Had he talked about messaging, time would have flown. With a promise to continue at a later date, the furry mentor saw Blitz's drooping eyelids, ended the chat and walked away.

Tired from the being's interminable mumbling, Blitz was drifting into a restless slumber when a whoosh shook him awake. Irritably, he concluded they had created the letter system to ensure he remained bushed during his stay at the Rainbow Bridge.

Hi, Blitzy:

Lars and I have been exchanging troubling letters about you. You know him. He's a worrier.

In my honest opinion he is right to worry a little. You guys may have met before we did, but I lived with you for almost two years, and I think I know you a little better.

Remember how you used to share with me your innermost secrets? I remember our chats as if it were yesterday. Some of your wild ideas could be worrisome; no use denying it.

I don't know what you are planning, but some things you've let escape and some questions you've asked point to trouble with a capital T. What worries me the most is you seem to think your plans affect only you. That's not so. Whatever you do at the Rainbow Bridge affects all of us.

Spirit Guide and Love Giver are really nice. And we–and when I say 'we' I mean all of us who live here–want to keep it that way. Remember I too have a big stake in a smooth meeting with our human parents. In fact, it's likely that when the time comes, we will receive them together. What's more, there may be four of us meeting our Daddy and Mommy.

I say there may be four of us meeting them because Daddy had a puppy when he was a young man. The puppy died of an illness within days of arriving at Daddy's house. Hansi looks almost like Lars, but he is a full-blooded German Shepherd. Daddy was very sad when Hansi died. He didn't tell you, and he didn't tell me–if I know Daddy–because he wouldn't have wanted to make us sad. But, Spirit Guide told me the story when I asked to see my first family.

Mommy also had a puppy when she was a young girl; a puppy she had to give away because his barking bothered some idiotic neighbor. She seldom tells anyone about it, but I'm a girl like her, and we girls keep many of our bad memories to ourselves. Spirit Guide also told me about

Mommy's puppy; the one she called Blackie. It's getting complicated, huh Blitzy?

The issue now is who will meet Daddy or Mommy, whoever comes first, and who will wait for the other one. Sometimes they split us up for the initial meeting so that our families feel welcome when they arrive, but it is still tough on the one who has to wait. In the case of Daddy's puppy and Mommy's puppy, that's a no-brainer. Hansi will be there for Daddy and Blackie will meet Mommy. But you and I may get split up. I suspect that I'll wait for Mommy because we are both girls and she was the one they called from the Rescue to help me out.

I don't know. It could go either way.

As you can see, plans for our reunion are sensitive. The least trouble will derail it. That's why I'm so concerned about what you may be trying to do. It bears repeating: I know you and I'm scared of how your mind works.

Don't be mad at me for being so honest with you. I want the best for us all.

A big kiss,

Maggie

Maggie's letter disturbed Blitz more than a scolding from Spirit Guide would have. She was smart and did not mince words. He guessed she learned to be that way when she lived with a cat in her former family; and he smiled at that thought. It had been a long time since he had let a dog's natural mistrust for cats dominate his thoughts.

For sure, he had to watch out for his older sister. She was seriously dangerous.

He had to cover his tracks better. He could not afford a slip up with Maggie watching him. And she would watch him like a hawk if she could. Good thing he was probably as invisible to Maggie as she was to him.

My dearest Big Sister:

I guess I deserve your scolding for all the times I let you down back on Earth. I remember that time when you were desperate to make water but Mommy and Daddy were out, and I told you they wouldn't get mad at you if you did it in the house. I swear I didn't want to get you in trouble. I just didn't want you to suffer so much holding it in, and I misread how they would react. When they yelled at you I was embarrassed I had let you down. I couldn't look at you without lowering my eyes and flattening my ears.

Look, the fact is that I am anxious about our human parents suffering for our deaths. I wish they knew we are all OK up here. With all the other things they have to worry about on Earth, it's unfair to have to worry about us as well.

But I don't want you to worry either about my getting us into trouble. I had my first talk about the rules with Spirit Guide just a little while ago. It was mainly about trust.

He said Love Giver lets us make our own decisions because he trusts we will try to be good. It's more like she hopes we'll be good, but he knows we are not perfect. Spirit Guide says there are very good reasons for the rules; usually having to do with hurting someone. It's when we are not good that he gets sad for us. So, yeah, there's a lot at stake. More than any punishment we could get.

So, Sis, I promise you I'll try to stop myself from doing anything that could get us in trouble, and not because they could punish us, but because we would punish ourselves when we see how sad Spirit Guide and Love Giver would get.

I scratch you behind the ear.

Your Blitzy

Blitz felt great relief when he sent the letter. He truly had resolved to be good and accept the fact that he would have to wait. Then, the little voice in his head reminded him he had failed to stick to good intentions before. After promising Maggie he'd behave, the best he could do was taking it one day at a time.

Love, promises, disappointment, pain; life was surely complicated. All this talk about emotions exhausted Blitz. He couldn't believe he had almost roped himself into dropping his plan. In the meantime, the little voice in his head was nagging him for being a wimp. Disappointed in himself, and confused about what to do next, he did not go back to his usual tree but dozed off near one of the brooks where he had stopped to read Maggie's letter. The brook's murmur was certainly relaxing.

FOURTEEN

Blitz awoke to the same sound he had fallen asleep to: the brook's gently running waters. It confused him at first, but much of the confusion wore off when he yawned, stretched and resumed the trek Maggie's letter had interrupted. The treks themselves did not commit him to a particular course of action. They would not be bad in themselves if he did not use them for a bad purpose. Realizing it could go either way was healthy. It was amazing how free he felt.

For the first time he could really enjoy the beautiful scenery: gorgeous trees, calming brooks and majestic rocks. For instance, there was a rounded obelisk next to an imposing willow just over to his left. He smiled when considering Spirit Guide's potential ruse. For all he knew, he Lars and Maggie were close by. Maybe Spirit Guide would do something like that to keep better track of his wards; to exert better control.

No matter. His spirit was no longer weighed down with dishonorable intentions. Or, was it?

What if Spirit Guide was a control freak and the purpose for making them invisible to each other was evil? Blitz dropped that line of thought like a hot potato. He was doing it again. There was a thin line between his resolve to be good and the temptation to keep looking for a way to let his human parents know he, Maggie and Lars were OK. He shook his ears. He needed to discard dangerous thoughts.

Stopping after a few more steps, he looked back at the stone near the tree. His thoughts drifted to how clever Spirit Guide would be had he concocted such a deception for truly good reasons. It actually made sense.

He let his imagination run wild just for fun. How could they make something invisible? Was there a magic trick? And, if they were truly invisible, why was he able to see the brown dog go through the wall? Wait! It might have to do with the wall; something that happens only when you are crossing it.

Thoroughly distracted, he ran into a tree. He had to be more careful. Hold on! When he bumped into the wall, it didn't hurt. But this time, he had felt his nose hit a hard tree. It made him question the nature of the wall and the nature of the trees; their purposes. Why would colliding with a tree hurt, but bumping into the invisible wall would not? Could it be...?

A whoosh shook him off his daydream.

My dear little Blitz:

Maybe I was too rough on you. I did not want to make you feel bad about your scheming nature. There are things we can't change.

I love you just the way you are. Don't change because this old lady is afraid you'd get her in trouble. Keep being your wonderful self; the same guy who comforted me when my first family threw me out.

Knowing you were there, feeling you curled up against me went a long way to making my sadness bearable. I've forgotten to say how grateful I am for sharing with me the place that had been only yours. You are great, and I love you so much, little brother.

Run your crazy ideas by me and I'll help you make sense of them. You know Lars and I have your back.

I let him read my letter to you and his face turned serious. It was he who asked if I hadn't been too rough on you. He made me see how my words could have hurt you. So I told him I would write you again to say I'm sorry if I hurt your feelings.

If it will keep you out of trouble, you can use me as a sounding board.

I love you very much.

Maggie

He had just finished Maggie's letter when he felt Spirit Guide's majestic presence next to him.

"I saw you reading a letter and I waited for you to finish. It's not nice to interrupt someone. Is everything OK?"

Blitz didn't know what to tell Spirit Guide. Revealing the nature of their correspondence might make his mentor mistrust him. Daddy had once talked about thinking on one's feet; coming up with an appropriate response when an event or a question surprises you.

"Everything is fine, Sir, it was a letter from Maggie. As usual her words were wise and deep. They made me space out."

"That's good, Blitz. We should always respect the counsel we get from folks who love us. It's part of the greatest principle here at the Rainbow Bridge. Love Giver's greatest gift to us is his love. I've tried to inspire all of you to do what's best; but, unlike him, I'm not perfect.

"I once was one of you, except I didn't have a human family while on Earth. The Rainbow Bridge was getting crowded and very complicated. So Love Giver asked several of us who would not have a reunion to help him. We try our best to shoulder many of his worries, but we could never be as perfectly loving as he is. But I digress. Are you ready for another session on the rules?"

"Of course, Sir, lay them on me!" Although he tried to sound flip, Spirit Guide's disclosure he had never had a human family had saddened him. No wonder the guy seemed out of touch with Blitz's feelings.

Spirit Guide could not help smiling at Blitz's spunky answer. The smile took Blitz by surprise. He would not be able to smile if, like his mentor, he didn't have the hope of a family reunion.

FIFTEEN

Waking up from another nap; this had to end! It seemed he would fall asleep following a rules talk. He was convinced Spirit Guide made him drowsy on purpose so he could reflect on the rules while he slept. If it were so, it was further proof Spirit Guide was very clever. Clever, yes, but it was getting annoying.

Accepting the hand he'd been dealt, Blitz moved on and took stock of the situation once more. His experiences had taught him a lot: someone or something opens the invisible wall for those who had a good reason to be in the forbidden area, like going to meet their loved ones; there is enough time to sneak through when someone else was entering or departing the zone; the wall remains closed while the meeting with loved ones goes on; there are places to hide in the forbidden zone; they only allow one reunion at a time, but the meetings are fast and the next one happens in quick succession; he could sneak in when the meeting was about to happen and was able to sneak out when the wall would open for the next reunion.

His last talk with Spirit Guide and Maggie's letter yielded new data. Sometimes, a reunion involved several companions, as humans were likely to have had more than one non-human friend during their lifetime. Daddy had never told him about Hansi and Blackie; probably to spare him from his sadness. There was also a possibility they could split up to receive Earth loved ones who arrived at different times. Spirit Guide was once one of them, which meant someone could get promoted to help Love Giver; but it also meant the mentor could think like them and be aware of all the tricks they could conceive. More significantly, his mentor did not have a human family to meet, which made him less able to understand Blitz's problems. For those reasons, it made sense they would keep members of the same family close together but invisible to each other, so Spirit Guide didn't have to waste time locating all who would have to be in the same greeting party. Boy, they were clever at the Rainbow Bridge!

Blitz's brain hurt with so much stuff he had to remember. Considering all this data, any one of his discoveries might be the key to knowing what goes on at the Rainbow Bridge.

Having a lot of data made him want even more. Time to keep moving! He got up to continue his treks to the wall, not because he knew how they would help figure things out, but because he needed the calming effect of their routine. And then, things got real.

Whoosh!

Dear Blitz:

Maggie told Blackie and me you were here. She also told you a little about us. Let me introduce ourselves.

When our Daddy was a young man and still in school, his father had six dogs at the same time. There was Pepe, Campeon, Lupe, Pedro, Andre and Antoine. His Daddy had gotten them from different places. He saved Pepe from mean kids who were throwing rocks at him; Campeon from the danger of guarding a bar in a bad neighborhood; and Lupe and Pedro from dying of hunger on the dusty streets of a foreign country. His mother then made his father get André and Antoine from a puppy mill. Since they were French Poodles, they got French names.

Our human dad loved them all, but he knew his father and his mother were responsible for them. He wanted someone who he could be responsible for on his own. That's why they got me.

They got me from a nearby puppy mill, so I was not in the best of health. I didn't last long. Spirit Guide told me Daddy was very sad when I left for the Rainbow Bridge. In fact, he was so sad that my memory stopped him from getting another one of us until he got you, many years afterwards. I too remember him crying when I left. The difference is I don't remember having had pain. I was so young I would not have known how to recognize it. But I do remember the feeling of loneliness when I no longer had our Daddy with me.

Frankly, I was glad that he and your human mom got you. It meant the pain had subsided enough for him to give love to someone else who needed love. And that was you.

I confess I was a little jealous at first, but Spirit Guide explained how we would all meet him when he came up here; just like the other six met his father when he arrived. But, I've always been afraid he'd forget me and I wouldn't have anyone to meet. What a terrible thought!

Later, Spirit Guide introduced me to Blackie, who is here with us and will continue this letter.

Hi, Blitz. It's me, Blackie.

We are in the same family because I lived with your Mommy when she was a young girl. I know it was a long time ago, but I'm hoping my Mommy told you about me and how we stayed together only a short time. They forced her to give me away because a neighbor complained I barked too much. But my next family didn't care for me as much as our human mommy did.

Like Maggie, I had two families. Unlike Maggie, my first Mommy did not want to give me away. So, I chose her as my permanent Mommy. She really cried a lot when they took me away, so I know she loved me, even though she was really young when it happened.

That's how Hansi and I came to be in the same family. Since your Daddy loves my Mommy I hope he won't mind my waiting for her, if I'm allowed. I have also been afraid Mommy will forget me and I won't have anyone to receive.

I'm glad Maggie wrote Hansi and me about you. We feel like we've known each other forever.

We love you, Blitz.

Blackie and Hansi

This was more than he bargained for. While he was happy to learn about Blackie and Hansi, their existence made his plans more difficult. On the plus side, their being here added huge amounts of love. To Blitz, that was a great thing. The trouble was he now had to deal with it. First things first though.

Dear Hansi and Blackie:

I am happy to meet you both. I didn't know about Hansi, probably because Daddy wanted to spare me from such a sad event. But he would often talk to me about his feelings, so I'm not surprised he loved you. Some people thought it strange he would talk to me, so he only did it when we were alone. People on Earth know very little about love.

Blackie, I didn't know about you either. But I'm also not surprised our human mom didn't tell me. She loved me and would not have wanted to make me sad with the story of how they forced her to give you away. Also, she did not like to talk about sentimental things; she was afraid people would laugh at her. I'm sure she would have told Daddy. She knew he would never laugh at her. When she told him about sad things he would hug her and keep her secrets because he loved her.

I know you've been waiting for them for a long time. But I hope you find comfort at the thought that someday you will again see the people you loved; the people who loved you. I hope to see you when our Daddy and Mommy come, but you'll understand why I hope it won't be too soon.

Please write me from time to time to let me know your thoughts. We are family and I love you.

I kiss your ears,

Blitz

SIXTEEN

Learning about Hansi and Blackie, plus what he knew about Maggie, Blitz put together an additional fact about the Rainbow Bridge: those who waited had a say about the humans they would meet at their reunions. It might be an important thing to talk about with Spirit Guide during the next chat. Who knew what morsel of information could be the key to the answers he needed?

As if he had read his mind his mind, Spirit Guide slid up from a patch of clouds on the right. Blitz spoke with him as if he were continuing the last conversation, no longer surprised his mentor would show up when he needed him.

"Can I talk to you about things that others tell me in their letters, Spirit Guide?"

Blitz saw the counselor's eyes grow wide and his head tilt as if he were thinking 'Uh oh! What's this guy up to now?'

"Sure Blitz, but please remember that we like to protect letter privacy. So please, be careful to not betray their trust."

Blitz loved Spirit Guide's answer. It confirmed what Lars had told him about being free to talk about anything in their letters. He thought that was great news, and something to add to his confirmed data list.

"I'm curious how we have a choice on what loved ones we wait for. How come we can wait for someone and not others?"

"That's a great question, my boy. But it's better to answer it with a story that may help you understand the answer better."

Here it goes, thought Blitz. This guy is going to unload a bunch of stuff on me. Daddy used to say the truth is easy to tell in simple words. Spirit Guide must be setting me up to introduce another rule.

"People on Earth don't really know what goes on at the Rainbow Bridge, so sometimes they make up stuff. Love Giver considered that among other things when he created what she calls 'free will:' people get to decide whether to be bad or good. Love Giver is happy when people choose to do good.

"Sometimes he lets people get a glimpse of what goes on here. He chooses to inspire special people who have great intuition and good intentions. It's funny how even they misinterpret his revelations. Yet, there was one time Earth people came close to the truth about the Rainbow Bridge.

"Long ago there were people called the Navajo, the Paiute, the Ute and the Pueblo. They lived in a simpler world and had time to reflect on things. These folks loved and respected their elders, recognizing they had lived many years and learned many things.

"Anyway, their elders had the time to sit around and think about things. That's when Love Giver decided she would give those who were good some real hope. So he inspired the old folks to visualize what goes on at the Rainbow Bridge. They almost got it right.

"The elders told their peoples that when persons died, they would arrive at a bridge. At that bridge, all the animals they had met would wait to lead to a good place the humans who had treated them with fairness and compassion.

"In reality, as you know, things are a little more complex. The main point is: if you are good to other beings, even those you consider less important than you, you'll go to the good place. Love Giver loves us all equally and wants everyone to go to the good place. And, since he gives everyone an opportunity to love their brother and sister animals, what happens is their choice."

Blitz stared at his mentor in silence and gave him one of those head tilts that meant he had more questions.

"That's great, Spirit Guide. But I have a question. Suppose my human parents arrive at different times. Who gets to meet them, Maggie, Hansi, Blackie or me?"

"That is something Love Giver decides, Blitz, according to what is in your hearts. She can see into people's hearts. More than anyone else, he can be fair."

Blitz thought the guy had done it again. He had given him another non-answer. He was about to return to the willow to reflect on what Spirit Guide had said when another question occurred to him. He turned toward the mentor.

"One more thing, Spirit Guide: is there also a bad place?"

"Of course there is also a bad place, Blitz. But it's not like the stories they tell on Earth. It is not a fiery place. It's much worse. Although we will talk more about it later, what makes it a bad place is the absence love."

SEVENTEEN

Instead of simplifying things, what Spirit Guide had told him made it more difficult to make a decision. Blitz was no longer sure messaging his family justified breaking a rule. The cost of skullduggery in the forbidden zone had just gone up, and could mess up the reunion. Did he really want to risk upsetting both Spirit Guide and Love Giver?

He had to decide soon; more to be prepared than to address the possibility of his humans' impending arrival. The longer he waited, the bigger the chance Spirit Guide would discover and stop his scheming. And the longer he waited, the higher the likelihood his humans would show up before he got a chance to message them, making the entire exercise meaningless. For starters, he couldn't continue to ask so many questions. So many questions could raise flags.

Continuing his exploration more out of habit than need, Blitz changed his tactics; stopping at each trek's midpoint as if he needed to rest. In reality, he'd use each stop to spot Spirit Guide's location, and to see if his mentor followed him. He also kept his eye on the wall so as not to miss its openings and closings.

Suddenly, he caught a shadow speeding toward the protective wall. Blitz saw the blur turn into a small Poodle. The little dog was running so fast Blitz thought she would crash against the outer layer.

The Bridge's enclosure parted just in time. When it did, Blitz began to pant rhythmically to determine how many breaths the wall would remain open. It closed on the sixth breath.

Would the wall always remain open for six breaths, or would it go slower or faster depending on other factors? Several hours and many other visitors later he would confirm the wall remained open for six of his gasps.

Calling it a day after the gap filling discovery, he paused at the brook that ran near his tree. He put his head into its clear water to relieve the mounting fatigue. When he took it out and shook off the wetness, he thought he saw shapes through the flying droplets. One of those shapes looked like Lars! Blitz sneered at his wild imagination as he curled up under the tree's canopy to claim his well deserved rest.

His eyelids about to shut, he found a familiar comfort under the willow's drooping branches and pointy leaves. He was beginning to think of the tree as 'home.' Sleep came fast and departed even faster.

Blitz's eyes snapped open. A torrent of thoughts cascading through his mind, he recalled bits and pieces of things Lars and Maggie had said in their letters. They lived by a pleasant brook. There were trees which resembled the willow they all remembered.

He summoned what Spirit Guide had told him about keeping together those who awaited people from the same family. It could not be a coincidence. Could it?

Rushing back to the brook, he plunged his head into the crystalline water once more. When he took it out and shook off the water, he looked around deliberately. Yes! He could see shapes through the water droplets. There were several silhouettes. One of them looked like Lars. The others could be Maggie, and even Hansi and Blackie. His heart was beating so hard! He had to sit and think about this. Was it enough proof?

Seeking reassurance, Blitz noticed a fallen leaf looked bigger, more defined through a droplet resting on its surface. He observed the same phenomenon on fallen twigs. They looked bigger through the water. What if Spirit Guide used cloud vapor to conceal them from each other? What if he could turn that vapor back into water? Could he then see the others? Was there another way?

He dunked his head again and shook the water off; this time trying to pinpoint a more exact location for the large shadow he thought was Lars. It seemed to be curled up near the tree trunk.

He had to know!

My dear Lars,

What are you doing right now? What do your surroundings look like?

Please let me know right away. Details are important.

Love,

Blitz

He replicated the dunking-shaking maneuver as the letter whoosh echoed. Through the water droplets he saw the big shape react to the sound. He waited with more than bated breath.

Dear Blitz,

Here I thought your letters could not get any weirder. I'm beginning to worry about you, but I'll indulge you.

I had just curled into a nap, next to my tree, when your letter arrived. The whoosh startled me. Prior to that I had taken a drink from a nearby brook and thought the water really tasted good.

So, there! Is that enough detail?

Love,

Lars

Lars' answer walloped Blitz's composure in the way a clapper strikes the inside of a bell. He could see them through the water's prism! He now knew what Spirit Guide had been keeping to himself. The whoosh, and the rush it brought, had finally proven to harbor the greatest secret at the Rainbow Bridge: how Spirit Guide hid them from each other. He could have jumped up and down with happiness were it not his antics might have alerted his powerful mentor.

What next? How would this discovery shape his plans?

Sleep would be impossible under the circumstances. Blitz decided to forego yet another nap.

He paced furiously under the willow until he sensed someone was looking at him. Turning his head in a robot-like slow motion, he locked eyes with Spirit Guide.

EIGHTEEN

"What's up, Blitz? You looked as if you were running away from fire ants, but I assure you we have none at the Rainbow Bridge." Gosh, that sounded as if the humorless Spirit Guide had told a joke. But, he had also asked a question that needed an answer; and it couldn't be a truthful answer.

Quick on the uptake, Blitz knew he had to buy time to come up with a satisfactory answer. "Yeah, and why is that? I thought everyone came to the Rainbow Bridge after they died. Shouldn't there be fire ants too?"

The rapid retort surprised Spirit Guide. The expression on his face told Blitz his buying-time reply had succeeded. "The Rainbow Bridge is a place where we wait at the end of our lives on Earth for those we loved and loved us back. Humans don't think of fire ants as companions. In fact, they can't get rid of them soon enough. It borders on terror, really." Spirit Guide's lips had curled up into an impish smile, but he quickly returned to his serious deportment.

The next answer needed to be well thought out, iron-clad; but first a bit of flattery. "Oh, I guess you are right, Spirit Guide."

"I'm seldom wrong, my boy. But don't let your fiery thoughts deflect my question." It must have been the fire ant pun that made Spirit Guide grin. "Why were you pacing so rapidly?"

Blitz countered with an artful dodge, something to keep Spirit Guide in the dark; but something that sounded plausible. "I had intended to take a nap, Spirit Guide. Instead, I foolishly plunged my head into the brook's water. The cold water cleared the cobwebs, all right. But it also kept me wide awake. I thought if I walked at a fast pace for a few minutes the air would dry me and I would get sleepy. Sorry. Is there a rule about pacing I broke?"

He knew Spirit Guide was hard to fool. Blitz didn't want to give him answers that were too clever. This one was close to insubordination. Smart aleck retorts might work temporarily, but risked increased suspicion. The furry mentor gave him a stern warning. "No, Blitz. If you had broken a rule, I'd let you know so fast your head would spin; not to mention other remedies I could apply."

Blitz accurately guessed lowering his head in contrition would make Spirit Guide regret the sharp comeback. "But no, my boy, I would never chastise you for accidently breaking a rule. Your furious pacing just seemed strange. That's all."

"Sorry, Sir. I know I'm playful and can sound flip, but I always follow rules to the best of my ability." He designed the response to put to rest any suspicion Spirit Guide might have. His mentor's next answer would determine if it had worked.

Not quite.

"OK, Blitz. I'll buy your explanation for now. But don't think you or anyone else can break the rules we've put together to make things run smoothly." Spirit Guide paused to let the caution sink in. His voice turned softer. "I really came to check on how you were doing, and whether you are getting used to us. It's important you are all happy while you wait for your loved ones."

Spirit Guide walked away slowly instead of rapidly disappearing into the fog, as he usually did. He seemed reluctant to depart and leave Blitz to further misunderstandings and possible misdeeds.

Blitz let out a stealthy sigh, knowing it had been a close call. But he shook off his worry. He had to think how his new discoveries could help him send a reassuring message to his human parents; or not.

So far his outward behavior seemed to have contained Spirit Guide's suspicious nature.

Resuming his treks, Blitz thought he needed the comfort and the time they bought him. Although it troubled him, he continued to keep an eye out for Spirit Guide. It was the prudent thing to do. Pausing at a trek's midpoint as if he were resting, he could look around innocently to spot his mentor.

NINETEEN

From the trek's midpoint on which he now sat, the multicolored Rainbow Bridge had become even more magnificent. To Blitz, the yellows had turned deeper, and the reds more dramatic. Maybe his mind was playing tricks.

He remembered he'd first mistaken it for a road on which someone had thrown a roof, but that was from afar. The colors emanating from the roof tiles had become brighter. And, although the interior accented its mystery, its darkness seemed welcoming, compelling; definitely not scary, sort of.

"Hello again, Blitz." Spirit Guide cut short his daydream.

It was disquieting his mentor had chosen this particular moment to come to him. Had he sensed he was troubled? For once, Blitz welcomed the interruption.

"Hi, Spirit Guide, I'm so happy to see you." The cheerfulness of Blitz's greeting pleased the mentor. It wasn't often new arrivals were happy to see him.

"Well, now! You seem to be in high spirits. I'm glad. I had been considering another chat about the rules. It's important to receive these counseling sessions in the spirit in which they are given, and at moments when you need them most. I've learned counsel is most effective when folks are approachable. What about having another talk right now; maybe one of the most important ones? Your aura told me you needed me badly. Am I right?"

It was creepy Spirit Guide could read him so accurately; so much for hoping he could hide things from him. "You are right, Spirit Guide. A little while ago I got a letter from Hansi and Blackie. It's their first letter to me and they went right to the point. They are worried Daddy and Mommy won't remember them and not reunite with them once they come from Earth. Is that possible?"

"Oh, little Blitzy, my talk about messaging might be overdue. I didn't think I would have to deal with it so early in your stay. But you are one of my brightest wards and I should have known you'd rush the schedule."

Blitz perked up at the reference to messaging.

"Do you remember writing Lars your Daddy had once 'talked' to someone he called 'God' asking him to help you?"

Spirit Guide's words froze Blitz's heart with fear. His mentor had mentioned something he'd written Lars. "But, I thought the stuff we wrote to each other was private, Spirit Guide!"

Seeing Spirit Guide's smile of reassurance at his alarm, Blitz feared the worst. Would his mentor now reveal he had read all his letters and discovered his trickery? He'd have to once again jump through hoops to protect his privacy and dispel any Spirit Guide suspicion.

"I can't read your letters, Blitz. Lars told me about it. He sensed you were troubled and wanted me to help you. As for privacy, it's an important part of the bargain Love Giver made with all of us. Your thoughts are yours alone until you turn them into action. We are not forewarned. Folks on Earth call it 'free will.' It's not difficult to understand. Love Giver teaches us by example, but does not force you to be good. She lets you make your own decisions.

"Some people will make bad choices. The consequence of making bad choices is not a place full of fire, as some folks on Earth believe. It's worse, and we touched on that once before. Those who make bad choices have to live with the knowledge they have hurt the being who gave them nothing but love. That absence of love is the worst feeling you can reflect on after you die, when it's nearly impossible to change."

Blitz felt the pall of guilt choke him. The feeling was very unpleasant. He couldn't begin to guess to what dastardly degree he may have disappointed Love Giver. There could be worse things than tricking Love Giver; but nothing came to mind.

Deep inside, he knew Love Giver had good reason to differentiate good from bad, and to leave the choice to those he loved. But this turn of events and revelations had an immediate effect on Blitz. His protective mechanism made him want to curl up into a tiny puppy, giving him a chance to deal with his failures with a fresh perspective after growing up. That's how he dealt with sadness and bad developments.

"In any case, Blitz. This chat is not about reading letters or even the difference between good and bad. It's about talking to Love Giver.

"Your Daddy and many other persons try to talk with the being they call 'God.' Some call it prayer. Prayer is a good thing, but unscrupulous people have taken advantage of its importance, saying folks can only talk to 'God' through them.

It's gotten so bad that people have hurt and killed others on account of those who claim to be a true intermediary.

"Those who misused the nature of prayer disappoint Love Giver. They had no reason to hurt her; someone who gave them only love. So your Daddy was right being sad those men he prayed with could not help you.

"And it's all so simple, my friend. By now you may have realized 'God' and Love Giver are the same being. The thing is, Love Giver is happy to listen to everyone she loves; and that's everyone, whether or not they do what he wants. Love Giver doesn't care how you come to him. She just hopes you do things according to the love he teaches by example.

"People ask Love Giver for many things. They do not understand things will happen as they are supposed to happen. No one lives on Earth forever. People do get sick, hurt and die. Other people hurt them and make them die. All Love Giver wants from people and other beings is that they love each other. He hopes they will let love guide them. It's such a simple formula, but their limited knowledge spoils things.

"The short and the long of it is they can ask Love Giver to help them. And he is always willing to listen because she loves them. Remember that, my Blitz. That's the most important rule."

"Wait, Spirit Guide. I'm confused. Sometimes you call Love Giver 'he' and other times 'she.' Until now, I have also used 'he' and 'she' indiscriminately to refer to Love giver; just like I heard you call him or her in the past. But, clear this up for me. What is Love Giver anyway, a 'he' or a 'she?'"

"The truth is… it doesn't matter, Blitz."

TWENTY

After Spirit Guide left in his usual downy cloud, Blitz knew he had a lot to think about. Somehow he knew this last chat would either solidify or change his plans.

He reached his favorite spot under the willow and let his exhaustion curl him up into a nap. Through the fog of his fatigue, he sensed this nap might be filled with those thoughts people called 'dreams.' His dreams were often jumbled and strange. Yet, Blitz knew he would always wake up seeing things in a different light.

The moment his eyelids rolled up, he ran to the spot where he had last chatted with Spirit Guide.

"Spirit Guide, where are you? I need to ask you something."

He felt his mentor standing by his side before he saw him.

"I kind of knew you'd want to continue our chat and ask questions about the things we talked about. That talk, my little Blitz, is usually the most important one; although not everyone is as perceptive as you. You really understood what I was telling you, right?"

"I think I did, Spirit Guide. And the reason I did is embarrassing."

Spirit Guide looked at Blitz with eyes filled with love; with the realization his efforts were paying dividends, as intended.

"You see, Spirit Guide, I was planning to do something bad, but for a good reason."

"That's the way many folks rationalize bad deeds, Blitz."

"No, I mean it. Do you remember all those times you saw me walking back and forth to the wall that stops us from getting to the Bridge? Remember you asked me what I was doing? Remember what I told you? Well, Spirit Guide, I was lying to you."

A spark of light showed in Spirit Guide's eyes. He truly loved this boy.

"Ever since I arrived I couldn't stand the thought of my human parents crying their eyes out, believing something bad had happened to me. I didn't want them to think my leaving for the Rainbow Bridge had been a bad thing. I was desperate to reassure them it was exactly the opposite. It was true that they would not be able to see me again on Earth. But they didn't know for sure they'd see me someday.

"I needed to let them know I was all right and that we would be together again. Waiting by the wall, I snuck through when someone entered it. It was scarier than I had thought. I was terrified I would not be able to return and you'd find out. I would hate to hurt your feelings."

"That is disappointing Blitz…"

"Wait, I'm not finished. I was also scared of disappointing Love Giver since the time you told me about her or him, whatever. I imagined all kinds of terrible punishments in terms of what I knew from living on Earth. The worst was: I never considered there was a simpler solution until you told me."

"And what was that, my boy?"

"I had not considered I could ask Love Giver to help me reassure my Mommy and Daddy."

Spirit Guide gave Blitz a smile that said: 'If I didn't know better, Blitz, I would say my job here is done.' Then he sighed as if saying: 'This boy gets it. But, I know I'm not yet off the hook.'

"Don't get angry Spirit Guide. There are one or two more things."

Spirit Guide half-closed his eyes and gave a mental groan. "I knew it! What else have you in mind?" His tone hit the lower notes, worrying as usual about the wild permutations Blitz's thinking could take.

"Do you remember when I told you I had put my head into the brook and shook it when I took it out? As I shook it, I saw shadows through the droplets; shadows that looked like Lars and Maggie and Hansi. They were all under my tree.

"Then I thought about something you had said about keeping those of us who waited close together so it would be easier to get us to the Rainbow Bridge when our loved ones arrived. I wrote Lars asking what he was doing, and he described something I saw through a water droplet."

"Oh, Blitz…"

"Wait, hear me out. I had a bad thought. I know what you and Love Giver do up here is guided by love, except for one thing. Many of us, like Hansi, spend a long time waiting for our loved ones.

"I know it's easier for you and Love Giver to control what happens by keeping us apart. But did you ever think it might also be cruel? Doesn't that go against Love Giver's nature?

"Blitzy, I assure you..."

"Hold on, Spirit Guide. I know you guys had the best intentions and never thought about the fact that what you were doing could hurt us..."

"Now you wait, Blitz." The words came out loud and angry; and sad at the same time. "I hope I did not mislead you thinking Love Giver had set up a system that could be cruel. She didn't. He asked me and the other Spirit Guides to handle the details of the meetings. It's my fault. I failed to think things through."

Blitz didn't know what to say and fell into a deep, poignant silence. He had not wanted to hurt Spirit Guide; nor had he sought his apology. Now, it was not only sad, but embarrassing.

"I'm sorry Spirit Guide."

"You don't have anything to be sorry about, Blitz. I messed up. I'll have to go to Love Giver and tell him."

"Hold on, Spirit Guide. I'm embarrassed to have made you realize you did something wrong. Please let me help make it better."

"How could you possibly help me make it better? I failed Love Giver."

"Love, Spirit Guide. You told me love was what Love Giver cared about. Sure, tell her you made a mistake. But also show him a way in which you can rectify your mistake with love."

Spirit Guide was in awe. Sure, Blitz was a rascal. But he was a bright and loving rascal. "Tell me, Blitz, how precisely would you have us fix it?"

The rascally Weimaraner held Spirit Guide's undivided attention while he explained his plan.

TWENTY ONE

The colors shooting off its roof were so bright they hurt the eyes. Around the Bridge, the yellow, red, green, and orange shooting stars cast multicolored shadows on the fluffy ground. They mystified those who waited; especially Blitz, who now walked into the Bridge's inside gloom.

He had to do it. It was the day. A moment ago he had felt strange forces moving him toward the wall. He sensed a bright energy carrying him through, just like he had seen the other dogs rush through the magic obstacle.

The others expected him to go through with it.

Little Hansi followed him at a distance; trembling with expectation. Would Daddy remember him too?

Blitz was both scared and happy. His eyelids fluttered and the pupils in his hazel eyes grew in size. The muscles on his face formed long wide lines. His tentative steps showed the fear in his heart.

The platform of soft clouds below brought him no comfort. When he first got to the Rainbow Bridge, he enjoyed running through its misty substance. Now, their vapor wrapped around his hopeful expression and formed droplets on his eyelashes. The droplets mixed into his tears. Yes, tears. He couldn't hold them back; like he couldn't stop shivering. His entire body shook, not in anticipation but like when it was cold.

His Rainbow Bridge family stood at the head of the crowd like cheerleaders rooting for the Blitz-Hansi team. They had gathered at the wall to send them off.

Maggie had chosen to linger at the Rainbow Bridge to wait for Mommy and accompany Blackie, who was terrified at the thought Mommy might not remember him when she saw him. Blitz's and Hansi's reunion could forecast what was in store for the Mommy reunion.

They stared at Blitz and Hansi. Their eyes also fell on those near them. It was the first time they could actually see each other. Someone in the crowd had said Blitz had made it possible. They said Blitz talked Spirit Guide–and someone murmured even Love Giver–into changing things for the better.

All eyes locked on the duo nearing the end of their journey; some with envy, some with concern. Two or three of the onlookers could not hide their joy, especially Lars, Maggie and Blackie.

Blitz did his best to postpone the moment of moments. He nurtured seemingly inconsequential thoughts to mask his fear. He wondered briefly why they called him Blitz. He knew the thing about how it meant "lightning" in German: and how Mommy liked to make those different sounds when she was angry, but also when she cuddled him. That entire line of thought would have to wait. Now was not the time.

He looked at Hansi over his shoulder. If he was scared in the Bridge's dark inside, how would his little brother fare. Blitz made an effort to smile at the little one, hoping he could see it in the dark.

The meeting was supposed to take place on the other side of the covered bridge. There were rumors it wasn't as pleasant there as it was on this side, but only rumors. No one was ever sure of anything on their side of the Rainbow Bridge.

Someone wrote him once he would have to run downhill when he got to the other end of the Bridge. That sounded legit. He vaguely recalled walking uphill toward the Bridge when he first arrived from earth. Running also made sense because it would be natural to want to run into the arms of the new arrival.

How many times had he woken up to the loud and strange sounds a reunion made? Each time he hoped it would be him, or even her, or even one of the little ones. Oh, no, he hoped it wouldn't be one of Daddy's little girls. He would have been ecstatic to see them again, but it was time for the older beings, not for the younger ones. A thunderclap outside the Bridge startled him, not registering it was the first time he'd heard one here. He should hurry.

Inside the Bridge it was not only dark but humid; a sensation he remembered from earth. Maybe that's why more droplets formed in his eyes. Who was he kidding? They were tears; tears which contrasted with the dryness in his tongue and the shortness of his breath. It had been such a long time, such a long wait.

His legs dragged on the Bridge's floor slats, making the trek even more difficult. How would they react when they saw him? Would they recognize him despite assurances that beings looked the same as the last time they had seen them?

The run downhill

He was glad he had constantly thought about *the last time;* that sad day when Mommy and Daddy cried as the doctor did what he had to do. It would help him remember what they both looked like. In his nervousness, Blitz's greatest fear now was forgetting what his human parents looked like in person; it had been so many years.

Light exploded. He had reached the end of the Bridge's dark tunnel. The other side was bright, just as he remembered, not multi-colored as where he now lived. The brightness hurt his eyes when it pierced the tears.

In the Weimaraner tradition, he flapped his ears so hard that the sound carried to the new arrival. The figure looked up from the bottom of the hill. Blitz saw Daddy look at him with distended eyes. His human dad's hands clasped, trembling and expectant.

He flapped his ears again; this time to draw the courage he needed to run downhill. They had never understood down there that he and the others with long ears shook them hard to mark an end, or a beginning. Yes, this was it. It was the end, or maybe the beginning. It was time. His legs took over and he sped downhill.

As he ran, he thought it didn't feel like such a long distance to the bottom of the hill. He put on more speed and made his dog sound; and he made it louder still. And the man looked up at him, his shaking lips opening midway between a smile and a sob. Extending his arms toward him, the man began to run uphill. And then Blitz heard him loud and clear. "Blitz! My little baby Blitz! Oh, my Blitz!"

And Blitz barked and jumped into his arms and licked his face wanting to use the human sounds he had learned with Spirit Guide to call him Daddy again and again; to say all the things he had wanted to say all these years… all these years.

The moment

"I always knew I would see you again. I think Mommy knew it too, but you know how stubborn and proud she could get. She would never admit it to anyone. But I knew."

Blitz tilted his head in the way he always did when he found something interesting or strange; or when he heard something he couldn't understand. Daddy saw it in his eyes.

He felt Daddy's arms around him and heard his soft words. He had missed those soft sounds. "Puppy, I was there the times Mommy wouldn't let you die. She helped the doctors save your life so many times. She was the strong and fearless one in the family; me, not so much. Where you were concerned, I was a big coward.

"Once, I was driving us back home after one of your surgeries. Mommy suddenly looked at you and yelled you weren't breathing. She screamed 'no!' and told me to drive back to the vet's clinic while she cried and caressed you and shook you.

"The clinic was closed by the time we got there. Both our hearts must have stopped beating at that moment. Sunk into a deep despair we didn't know what to do next. The clinic was very far away from the city. Mom was sobbing. 'Oh, God, no. Not my Blitzy.'

"In the car's rearview mirror I saw her face freeze. Suddenly, it lit up. You had moved and coughed, and frothy blood spewed out. It was good blood. It meant you were alive.

"Yes, I was there." Daddy's eyelids lowered and tears slid down his face. His voice turned deeper and more subdued. "I was there not only when they saved your life. I was also there when we told the vet he could put the needle in you. And I saw Mommy's face, and her terror, and her tears. I held her, and she held me just as tight."

"Daddy, stop it. You will cry. You never liked to cry. Remember how you used to say that men didn't cry?" The daddy sounds felt strange in his mouth. He would later think back to this moment and understand the astonishment on Daddy's face.

Daddy's eyes had opened wide and his lips shut tight. He could finally understand what Blitz said. And Blitz could understand everything Daddy said. The joy was so great that there was no room for other thoughts; even remembering that Mommy was now down there, all alone. What was worst: although she may suspect she would see them again, she would be despondent not knowing for certain. Mommy always liked to know for sure.

Despite the new human sounds in his voice box, Blitz had no words. It was a time for silence. He curled up next to Daddy and let out a sigh. This was a moment for hushed feelings. Daddy's arm around him told him so. Daddy slumped and buried his face in Blitz's neck. It felt warm and wet.

It was comfy like that, just like when he lived down there with his human parents. All the stuff Daddy had told him was running through his mind.

Unexpectedly, Blitz broke the magic of their embrace, the cycle of comfort.

"Wait, Daddy, I almost forgot." He looked behind and his eyes locked on Hansi. "I'm not alone here, Daddy."

Hansi took a tentative step closer, his little heart pounding in anticipation.

Blitz turned his head slowly, gazing at Hansi, praying Daddy would remember him. It would be disastrous for the little one's confidence if…

"Hansi! My little puppy Hansi! All these years I never lost hope I could see you again. No, that's not true; I knew I would see you again. There were so many things we could have done together. We would have so many stories to laugh about if only you had not left so soon."

"Oh, Daddy! All these years my only hope was that you'd remembered me. I would say to myself 'If only Daddy remembers me I will be the happiest puppy in the universe.'"

"How could I forget you, my little ball of fur?"

Three beings seemed to meld into one, with Daddy at the center; holding, caressing, crying and talking… all at once.

The journey

Blitz took the lead and asked the question he and Hansi were thinking about. "How, Daddy? What happened? How did you get here? Did it hurt?" Daddy was expecting the questions, and he told them everything they wanted to know. Better yet, he told them all the while he felt happy knowing he would be here with them for good. Daddy had always known.

A strange sensation came upon them. As if on cue, they got up and walked uphill toward a light to the right of the Rainbow Bridge.

They didn't consciously know where they were going, but it felt good walking together. That was all that mattered right now. Their steps were soft and evenly spaced. Their feet moved slowly but comfortably uphill, the way you feel when you've done it before; like when they used to go on walks to the pond in the old neighborhood.

Daddy had things to do, and Blitz and Hansi instinctively knew they were supposed to stay by his side. Their smiling eyes met and held, basking in the happiness of the moment; silently assuring one another that everything was finally all right. It was a new feeling, but it was an old feeling too. They were together.

The mist broke abruptly. They were not alone anymore. Others who had come before them were there. They embraced and cried tears of happiness. Humans had daddies and mommies of their own, and siblings and people they had loved down on earth.

Blitz and Hansi felt a tinge of jealousy as their human embraced others. But they noticed Daddy looking for them out of the corner of his eye, even while others hugged him. It would be fine. Daddy loved others, but he also loved them. It would, indeed, be fine.

ABOUT THE AUTHOR

My name is Dan Santos and I like to tell stories.

I've traveled to many places and seen incredible things, beautiful people, unbelievable goodness and despicable evil in all their manifestations. These places, people and things might go unnoticed unless someone tells others about them. That's what I do, hoping to transport readers from their everyday reality to a different world.

My writing reflects years of serving my country and my family as a soldier, diplomat, son, husband, father and human companion. All these I've done with great intensity because I believe there is no other way to live life.

It was hard to write about my best friend Blitz. The tears wouldn't let me. I lived his love and his pain and imagined his angst at getting to the Rainbow Bridge all alone. He was beautiful, intelligent and brave; so brave he would be more concerned about the suffering of those he left behind than about his own pain. And he was also a rascal; the kind who would jump through hoops to makes us laugh and play with him. I regret the references to Daddy's good traits seem self-serving, but we all know our dogs think the world of us.

I live in the house he died, so I feel his presence everywhere, from the source of Maryland's Rock Creek where he played hide and seek with the deer, to the family room from which he left us. I firmly believe he's waiting for us, and that I will see him again someday.

ACKNOWLEDGEMENTS

Telling the story of someone you loved is fraught with emotional dangers, self-doubt and the need to excel at this craft for his sake. It hurts to think of him as one more protagonist; a product of character development and writing techniques. But the worst is having to dilute and alter his real personality to fit a plot.

It was hard for me to write "Letters from Blitz," but it was doubly hard for people who knew Blitz to read it. And for that I thank my Beta Readers, who all knew and loved Blitz. I'm tempted to go name by name, but it would take many more pages than we have available.

Hundreds of people in three continents loved Blitz. Some took care of his health and others just enjoyed his company. My gratitude goes to those who were kind to our fur baby, in particular Chet Anderson, DVM, who kept him as healthy as possible; and to Tom Knott, owner of Tomar Kennels, who befriended us and answered our many questions throughout his life.

A heartfelt thanks to my editing team for the long hours spent making sure this novella is as good as it can be.

Most importantly, I thank the readers. They are worth all of this, and more.

OTHER BOOKS BY THIS AUTHOR

"Insurrection: Appalachian Command"

Americans fight the surviving Navy admiral who usurps the government when international terrorists blow up the White House and the Capitol, slaughtering the president and most high level officials.

Reluctantly paired, a man and a woman kidnap the dictator's wife to use as leverage for the release of their comrades. He a former Army Ranger and she a Military Police officer find common ground in their hatred for the dictator, and their need to avenge their families. Terrorists and the dictator's troops chase them through the Potomac River's wilderness. Unpredictable feelings for each other make their task harder.

This is the first of three episodes of the Insurrection Series.

"Insurrection: Mile High Blood"

Parting angry at each other after a disastrous mission, the freedom fighter commander sends them their separate ways; Kate to protect an interim civilian president the rebels elected and Jude to carry out a commando mission.

The Chinese forces occupying the US West Coast kidnap Kate and the president. Jude is called to free them; a task that will take him from Colorado to California in a mad helicopter and ground chase. The fight against elite Marines from the People's Liberation Army is bloody and costly.

This is the second of three episodes of the Insurrection Series.

"Insurrection: Tiger Legion"

After a daring landing at a Chinese controlled base, Jude's commandos infiltrate a naval base and attempt to free the rebel president.

In the aftermath of the raid on the naval base, Jude and Kate learn the identity and location of the terrorist leader responsible for the deaths of their families.

What started as a resistance military operation in the States turns into a risky and bloody international chase.

This is the third of three episodes of the Insurrection Series.

Coming Soon

"El Polizón" (Provisional Title)

The author's first novel in Spanish tells the early 1900s story of a stowaway who joins a feared Neapolitan organized crime family to assassinate a prominent American figure.